"Lea is gone. I'm learning to accept that. I thought I had nothing I could ask you that would help. You can't bring back her body. Then I thought about her spirit.

"This is my only request. That you make four whirligigs, of a girl that looks like Lea. Put her name on them. Then set them up in Washington, California, Florida, and Maine—the corners of the United States. Let people all over the country receive joy from her even though she's gone. You make the smiles that she would have made. It's the only thing you can do for me." She exhaled. "That's what I ask."

She pulled something else out of her purse. "I bought him a Greyhound bus pass. Good for forty-five days. He can go anywhere."

Miss Gill repeated that restitutions weren't imposed, but accepted voluntarily by the offender. Brent's parents raised one objection after another, from his commitment to the emergency room to his need for his family, his nonexistent carpentry skills, and the cruel and unusual conditions of bus travel. Brent was oblivious of the arguing. In the quiet storm cellar of his mind, he pondered the proposal. Strange as it was, it would get him away from Chicago, his parents, and his recent past. It would also give him a chance to do penance. He'd never traveled on his own before. The idea held sudden appeal. He smiled inside. He cleared his throat. Then he spoke the words, "I'll do it."

Whirligig

Whirligig

Paul Fleischman

SCHOLASTIC INC.
New York Toronto London Auckland Sydney
Mexico City New Delhi Hong Kong Buenos Aires

For Honey and for Pearl

Contents

Party Time   3

Weeksboro, Maine   19

The Afterlife   33

Miami, Florida   55

Twinkle Twinkle Little Star   63

Bellevue, Washington   76

Apprentices   86

San Diego, California   102

"Everybody Swing!"   115

Whirligig

Party Time

Brent turned toward his clock. It was five thirty-five. He hated the hours before a party. A nervous energy whipped back and forth inside him. He focused again on the computer's screen and careened through the video game's dark passages, firing at everything speeding toward him, borne along by the never-ending music.

"Brent!"

His mother's voice echoed up the stairs. Brent paused the game. The firing and explosions ceased as if a window had been closed on a war.

"Dinner!"

"All right."

He played on, chewing up the minutes that stretched

before seven o'clock. Why couldn't you fast-forward through time the way you could with a video? He flicked another glance at the clock. Five forty-one. Real time was a drag.

He went downstairs. His parents had started eating. When they'd moved to Chicago a few months before, they'd suddenly begun dining in the kitchen, where they'd put a small TV. Brent served himself at the counter, then took his stool at the island and watched with his parents.

The Friday sports news was on, annotated by his father's grunts and snorts. Brent had learned to judge his mood from these. He reconnoitered his father's long, handsome face and studied the wrinkles, fine as if scratched in with a burin, feeding into his eyes. The promotion within his car-rental company had rescued them from Atlanta's heat, put Brent into a private school, bank-rolled Brent's mother's furniture-buying spree, but hadn't seemed to improve his own spirits. The caustic complaints about work had begun again. Lately, Brent had begun to feel sorry for him.

The news ended. His father reached for the remote, which Brent's mother always put to the right of his fork when setting their places. He dodged commercials, serving the rest of the family a finely ground visual hash. Switching the control to his left hand so as to take a bite, he inopportunely dropped it when the screen showed the victims of an African famine. A child crawling with flies was wailing. Brent's father scrambled for the remote. A white woman now faced the camera. "This tragedy—" she began, then was cut off.

"Let's go there for our next vacation," said Brent's mother. The remark drew no comment.

"I'm going to a party tonight," Brent spoke up.

His father dismissed from the screen a male newscaster, then a woman selling detergent. Brent found himself thinking of his parents' former spouses.

"I wish I was," said his mother.

All three watched a commercial for the new Jaguar.

"What do you say, Brent?" said his father. "Nice lines, huh?"

"Very nice," Brent replied.

He examined his father's words for signs that a Jaguar might now be in reach with his new salary. He imagined himself driving it, observed by the assembled student body, adding to the daydream a Calvin Klein shirt from the advertisement that followed. He put his dishes in the sink.

"Write down where you'll be," said his mother.

He skipped upstairs and showered, scrubbing himself with medical thoroughness. Though he was in his junior year, he still only had whiskers on his upper lip and chin. He shaved his whole face anyway, then applied aftershave. He put on deodorant and gargled with mouthwash. Taking his comb, he parted his straight blond hair down the middle, confronted the mirror, then combed it straight back, like the models in *GQ*. He worked in the mousse, imagining the hands raking his hair were Brianna's. Next he inspected his left ear's gold earring. At his school in Atlanta, it had been the right ear. Likewise in Connecticut. But at the Montfort School, in the western suburbs of Chicago, it was the left. His father's corporate climb had demanded four moves in the past seven years. Earrings were one of the first things Brent checked.

He returned to his room and flipped on the radio. Discerning what stations were considered cool was another of his moving-in tasks. No spell-chanting shaman knew better the importance of precise adherence to tradition. And keeping the right music flowing, using headphones between house and car, was as vital as maintaining a sacred flame. With the room now prepared, Brent set about dressing. It was May and no longer rib-rattling cold. He considered his large collection of T-shirts, weighing their logos, color, and condition. To impress without risking being made fun of was his mission, the latter especially important in the case of a party at Chaz's. Especially when you hadn't actually been invited.

He chose khakis and his Chicago Bulls T-shirt. He attached his wallet chain to a belt loop, tucked the wallet in his back pocket, then couldn't decide whether or not to wear his Vuarnet sunglasses. He finally stuck them in his shirt pocket as a compromise, then looked at the clock. It was six-thirty—still too early to leave. For half an hour he played video games, losing all of his lives in short order, the radio booming over the games' noise, his mind elsewhere. At seven he took off.

He drove to Jonathan's and honked. His friend bounded out, lanky and loose-jointed as a clown, wearing a Cubs cap backward and a pair of shredded jeans. Instantly, Brent regretted the choice of his neatly ironed khakis. They drove off.

"So how come you need a ride?" Brent asked.

"Forgot to pay my car insurance," said Jonathan. "My dad took the car for a month. 'There are consequences for our acts, my boy.' Like having to show up in your Studebaker instead of my Mazda MX-6."

"It's a Chevy, not a *Studebaker*."

Jonathan winced wearily. "No kidding."

A sense of humor was a luxury that Brent had never been able to afford. He was always the new kid, stumbling through the maze, never quite rich or good-looking or athletic enough to join the elite. Unless he played his cards right at the party tonight.

"So how do you get there?"

"Get on 355," said Jonathan. "I'll show you."

Brent drove through Glen Ellyn's maple-lined streets. Chaz lived all the way across the city, in Wilmette, on the lake. Montfort drew from all of Chicago. It was Brent's first private school. He'd cheered when he'd heard that his father would be making enough money to afford the tuition. Then, when they'd moved from Atlanta in March, he'd found that, measured against his new peers, he was suddenly a lot poorer than before. Getting any respect at Montfort was going to be like climbing a glass mountain.

"Get on the East-West Tollway," said Jonathan. The new song by Rat Trap was on the radio. He turned it up until the dashboard vibrated. "Then we'll take the Tri-State north. Then we'll cut over. I'll tell you where."

"And you're sure it's okay, me coming?"

"Trust me! I'm *his* friend. You're *my* friend. Therefore, you and Chaz are friends. As was proven by theorem 50 in chapter 6. Stop worrying! It's party time!"

Jumping from one freeway to another, they zigzagged across Chicago. Brent had his doubts about Jonathan's logic. But at least he was certain Brianna would be there. This was a chance to be with her without risking actually asking her out, to be seen with her, to make a statement. To take the next step. Maybe more than one.

They found the house, clustered with cars as if it were a magnet. Cherokee, Honda, BMW, another Cherokee. Brent knew all their models and prices. Judging by the crowd, he figured they were on the late side, which was fine. It gave the impression he had other, more important things on his schedule.

He parked and put on his headphones. They approached the stone house. It was vast and turreted, looming above them like a castle. Brent reached for the knocker, but Jonathan opened the door as if it were his own.

"Hey, it's a party. Remember?"

Inside, the rooms seemed too large, the ceilings too high. Brent felt out of scale. No one seemed to be around. He trailed Jonathan through the labyrinth, at last emerging onto the back patio. Music was booming from a sound system to their right. Below them, in the tennis court and on the grass and inside the gazebo, lounged the cream of the junior class. Brent felt he'd gained a glimpse of Olympus.

It was dusk. They wandered toward the others. Then Brent noticed something. He grabbed his friend's arm.

"Is there a dress code or something?"

Jonathan stopped. Then he saw it too. Everybody was wearing either all white or all black.

"Jesus!" Jonathan smacked his head, then grinned. "Forgot again."

"Forgot what?" Brent knew the panic had shown in his voice.

"We were supposed to wear white or black, like chess pieces. Chaz has some big party game dreamed up."

Brent glared at his friend. He felt he'd been tricked. Fury rose up in him from a deep well. He'd been a head-banger as a toddler and still threw tantrums when he didn't get his way. He knew he couldn't afford a tirade here. He pulled off his headphones and tried to form his reply.

"Relax," said Jonathan. "Chaz always has a theme. Check out the tennis court. It's a big chessboard. Must have used chalk. He loves this kind of thing. He's in Drama Club. Figures." He eyed Brent. "Don't sweat it."

He moved on, robbing Brent of his lines. Without Jonathan next to him, Brent felt conspicuous. Everything about the party made him nervous. Then the thought hit him that he could leave. He stuck out enough already without the added business of the clothes. This was the time, before the party game started, whatever it was. Down on the tennis court, two figures in white were rollerblading. He debated, teetered toward flight, started to leave—then sighted Brianna. The balance swung. He trotted and caught up with Jonathan, walking beside him as if nothing had happened. Then each felt a hand on his shoulder. It was Chaz.

"A yellow shirt and blue jeans?" he inquired. He affected the headmaster's English accent, sternly surveying Jonathan. He was tall and long-jawed, his sandy curls topped by a gold crown. "Really, Mr. Kovitz. This will lower your grade. Learning to follow directions is vital both to your success at Montfort and in the wider world beyond. Regardless of what pathetic, godforsaken piece of it you occupy."

Jonathan smirked. "I thought school was *over*." He viewed Chaz's crown and fingered his black cape. "Not to mention the Middle Ages. Anyway, I don't have a car at the moment, so Brent here drove me. I figured you could use an extra pawn or two."

Chaz took stock of Brent's catsup-red Bulls shirt. "Points off," he said. He dropped the accent. "Brent Bishop, right?"

Brent nodded his head.

"Bishop, like the chess piece," Chaz mused. "Let's see if he moves back and forth diagonally, the way a bishop should."

He stood behind Brent, put both hands on his shoulders, and guided him toward the left. Brent resisted at first, them complied, allowing himself to be treated like a toy, hating his helplessness. Abruptly, Chaz reversed direction, pulling Brent stumbling backward.

"Works fine to the left. Let's try the right."

People were watching. Brent felt like slugging Chaz, but knew his tormentor was taller, more muscled, and the de facto ruler of their class besides. If Chaz said that easy-listening music was hip, then it was. Losing his cool here would be suicide.

"Seems to be in good working order," said Chaz. He stopped, then turned Brent to the left. "Bishop to drinks table," he called out in chess-move fashion. Struggling not to trip, Brent was marched across the grass, through a circle of girls, and up to the table. He felt Chaz's hands release him and prayed his host would vanish. He did.

He replaced his headphones to help shut out the scene and stood staring, dazed, at the bottles before him. He felt as if he were still onstage. Playing to his audience and his own need, he poured himself a scotch and soda, heavy on the former. He added ice and sipped it quickly, feeling it run through him like a river of lava. Discreetly, he scouted the territory. The smell of pot smoke reached his nostrils. He spotted Jonathan in a group of boys on the lawn and headed that way.

The talk was of the Cubs. Brent marveled that people could publicly root for such perennial losers. The Bulls in basketball were different. They won. Both he and his father had bought Bulls shirts their first week in Chicago. His own stood out less among the whites and blacks as darkness fell. Then lights came on above the tennis court and inside the gazebo.

"The human chess game will commence in thirty minutes!" Chaz announced from the patio.

"Should be interesting," said the boy next to Brent.

The subject switched to hockey. Brent pretended to listen, sipping his drink and watching Brianna. He wanted to catch her alone. At the moment, she was talking with two other girls. She was drinking a beer and had a sullen look, her wavy blond hair reaching down her black dress like a hanging garden. His knowledge of her was sketchy. In his two months at Montfort he'd learned that she'd recently broken up with someone, that she stood near the top of the pecking order, and that her father, rumor had it, was worth a hundred million. He also knew, for a fact, that she was gorgeous. Having her for a girlfriend would mean instant respect. And why shouldn't she like him? He was tall, a little skinny perhaps, a bit uncoordinated, but reasonably handsome, with a square chin and no braces or acne. She was probably sick of the same old faces. She'd smiled at him off and on when they passed. They'd been assigned to the same group project in history. Making use of his newcomer status, he'd often asked her questions about Chicago, offering in return his services in math, his best subject. She hadn't taken him up on it as yet, but finals were coming. He had hopes.

He made another drink and returned, his nerves pleasantly numbed by the scotch. He took off his headphones. He was feeling more comfortable, proud of the fact that he could hold hard liquor. On the patio, Chaz had taken off the rap and put on French-sounding accordion music. It was so corny it was cool, and somehow fit the moment: a spring evening, the air warm at last, the leaves thrusting from the trees again and crowding out the sky. A faint breeze stirred the greenery.

Around Brent, the talk turned to cars, then gradually focused on Porsches. He heard his cue and roused himself.

"The 4-S really flies," he volunteered. "But tons of repairs. Always in the shop. Don't even say the word *Porsche* to my dad."

"He drives one?" asked Jonathan. "I always see him in that Continental."

"Back in Atlanta," said Brent. "Finally sold it." It was the sort of lie that would never be found out, the sort he'd drawn on often. Moving had at least that one advantage. Over the years, he'd grown adept at creating alternate pasts for himself. He glanced to his right and was returned to the present. Brianna was crossing the grass, alone.

He slipped from his group and hurried his steps to intercept her.

"Hi," he said.

She looked startled. She hadn't seen him in the shadows. "Hi," she replied flatly, then moved on.

He strode beside her briskly to keep up. "So who are you in the chess game?"

She reached the drinks table and poured herself some vodka. "Beats me."

She added tonic to her cup. He added scotch to his and sipped it. He lifted the top off the ice bucket for her. She ignored the gesture and walked away. He followed, emboldened by the alcohol to try to overcome her coolness.

"That history test was deadly," he offered.

"Sure was."

He tried to fight through the accordion music and the fog in his brain to find something to say, unaware she was headed for the crowded gazebo. He sipped his drink.

"If you need any help in math—"

Brianna stopped short, squeezed her eyes shut, then wheeled and screamed, "Stop hanging all over me!"

They were well lit by the light in the gazebo, where Chaz was giving a waltzing lesson. All heads turned toward Brianna and Brent. Conversation stopped.

"You're like a leech or something! Get off of me! Can't you take a hint? Go bother someone else! And that goes for at school too!"

There was silence but for the accordion's cheery tune. Brianna stormed up the gazebo's steps and disappeared into the crowd.

Brent stood, brain and limbs paralyzed, as if turned to stone by her curse. He'd never been in such a situation and had no ready response. The music and the black and white figures facing him made him wonder if he was dreaming.

"Been rehearsing that scene long?" asked Chaz for all to hear. "Drama Club needs you."

There was laughter at this. Brent's thoughts tilted crazily. He pictured them all repeating the scene to their friends, replaying it like the sports highlights, guffawing over it at the twenty-year reunion. He turned, desperate to get out of the light's glare, and started toward the shadows. Bounding down the steps, Chaz cut him off and placed both hands on his shoulders.

"Bishop to penalty bench," he called loudly. "Ten minutes, for sexual harassment."

More laughs. He aimed Brent toward a stone bench. The hated grip on his shoulders again, the public humiliation, the snickers, the alcohol, all mixed and detonated inside Brent. He stopped, whirled, throwing off Chaz's hands, and swung with all his might.

"Jesus!" came from the gazebo.

The blow missed Chaz's face, scraping his ear. Both he and Brent stood in shock, caught off guard, breathless. Chaz's crown had fallen off. Brent aimed a ferocious kick at it, connected, sent it spinning over the grass, then turned and stumbled toward the patio, alone.

"Calling Miss Manners," someone shouted out.

"Tell her it's an emergency."

"Y'all come back, Georgia boy."

He entered the house, his thoughts swirling. He took a wrong turn, passed through the dining room twice, kicked a wall in frustration, then charged down a hall and found the front door. He left it standing open behind him and steamed toward his car like a torpedo. Jonathan could find another ride home.

He got in and peeled out. His mind was a wreckage of sound bites and images from the last five minutes, endlessly repeating, shuffled, overlapping. It didn't seem real, but he knew it was. The consequences would be real as well. He was a leper now. No one would go near him. Certainly no girl. He'd destroyed himself.

He shot up an entrance ramp. "He *forgot to tell me* about the stupid clothes!" he yelled, and the tantrum began. "Some stupid, idiotic, goddamn friend!" He shouted out the catalog of the night's injustices, rained punishments on his enemies, wailed at his disappointments and deprivations. The flood of words seemed to bear him down the road. His head reeled with drink and despair. Then he saw that he'd gotten on the wrong expressway. This was 94. They'd come on 294, or so he thought. He rummaged hopelessly through his memory, trying to recall their route. He'd let Jonathan guide him and hadn't paid attention. He fumbled, opened the glove compartment, and let loose a landslide of cassettes. He felt around with his hand. No map. He was nearing Skokie. He began to get nervous. He wondered where 94 led. Then mile by mile the uneasiness passed. He felt strangely unconcerned. He realized that he really didn't care where he was going. Why should he? His life was a house that had burned to the ground. What was there to go back to?

He drove on, weaving slightly, aware that every car but his had a destination. He felt spent, emptied of all will. He was beyond tantrums. Instead, a measured voice began broadcasting within him, soft and unexpected, like a warm wind out of season.

There's no need to go home, said the voice. *No need to go back to school on Monday. No need to go there ever again.*

Ahead, car lights hurtled toward him just as in a video game. He was in the fast lane, steering between the white lights on his left and the reds on his right.

There's no need to feel pain. You've already felt enough.

The driver beside him honked when Brent drifted into his lane. Brent ignored him.

No need to let them hurt you again.

The voice flowed through his veins like morphine. He wove between the lights, hypnotized.

You have the power to stop the hurting.

He removed his hands experimentally from the steering wheel for a moment.

No need to be a pawn.

He put his hands back. The driver beside him honked once more, then slid several lanes over and sped up.

They are the pawns. You are a king.

He took his hands delicately off the wheel again.

You have a king's absolute power within you.

He held his hands in midair for several seconds. They shook slightly. Gradually, he lowered them and laid them lightly on his thighs. He stared blankly at the lights before him.

You have absolute power over your own life.

He saw that the car was drifting to the left. He felt his hands jerk, but kept them on his thighs.

You have the power to end your life. Now.

Very slowly, he closed his eyes.

Weeksboro, Maine

"**W**ould you mind telling me where we're going?"

"To a motorboat waiting in a cove," said Alexandra, "ready to take us to a French duke's estate on one of Maine's countless islands, there to join his harem."

"Dream on." I bumped her off the shoveled sidewalk and into the snow. "I'm serious."

"C'est une surprise," said Alexandra.

"You know I'm taking German."

"I also know you're brilliant enough to figure it out."

"And that I hate surprises."

"Honestly, Steph. Relax!"

The clearest winter days are the coldest. I gave my scarf a third and nearly fatal wrap around my neck.

"It's too freezing outside for ouija walking." An Alexandra invention in which you walk without any conscious plan, letting your feet go where they will.

"We're not going ouija walking," she said.

"The Nook is closed Sundays, so we can't steal scenes." Another of her amusements, consisting of ordering something at Weeksboro's one restaurant, listening to the people at the neighboring table, then talking about what *they're* talking about—carburetors, hysterectomies—completely ignoring them when they stare at you.

"We're not heading toward the Nook, as you can plainly see, *chère*."

We passed the Town Hall, fanged with icicles, and turned down Beech Street. "So where *are* we going?"

"Out to the point, near Pam McQuillen's. To throw a lifeline to a friend in distress."

"What friend?"

Alexandra smiled. "You."

I stopped, but she didn't. I caught up, skidding on the ice. "What are you talking about?"

She sighed, producing a cloud of vapor. "You don't like surprises. You like certainties. Facts. An extremely dangerous side effect of having marine biologists for parents. So let's look at the facts. First, we're eighth-graders. We're in our biological prime. In many cultures around the world we'd already be married and bearing children. Soon our beauty will fade. Very soon. Just look at Sheila

Sperl's older sister. Second, three weeks and six days ago, Trevor and I pledged our love to each other. Third, you remain unattached, as you've been all two and a half years of middle school. Fourth, it's the Christmas holidays, a time known to be especially painful for single people like yourself. Fifth and last, and most important, we've been best friends ever since nursery school. Who else but me has written you a birthday poem for six straight years? And who else besides you shows up at the Great Books discussion group I started? I don't want this to come between us, Steph. We have to find you a boyfriend."

We turned down Bolton Road. I was stunned.

"What have you got waiting out there?" I pictured a selection of boys tied to trees and penned naked in cages. "And who says I even want a boyfriend?"

"If you won't say it, then I will." Alexandra pulled her cap over her ears. "Communing with the urchins and eels in your aquariums can't be totally satisfying. It's time to move up to warm-blooded creatures. Boys, I'll admit, don't satisfy all needs. It's difficult to discuss Jane Austen with Trevor. Extremely difficult. That's why I value you. But there are some things males do awfully well."

"Like rape. Warfare. Water pollution . . ."

"And some things that you could do to attract them. Letting your hair grow out for one. Show me one *Playboy* model who looks like she gets her hair done by the U.S.

Marines. Long hair is mesmerizing to male humans. *This* is the kind of science you should be studying."

"Long hair is a hassle."

"*Life* is a hassle. *La vie est dure.* But it's worth it, right? You could also stoop to using makeup. Eyeliner. Blush. Something on your lips."

"And look like some washed-up Hollywood star on the cover of the *National Enquirer*?"

I could see Alexandra roll her eyes. "Didn't we have this exact discussion at sailing camp last summer? I'm telling you, the natural windblown look won't get you very far. It's strictly for the homeless and war refugees." She sighed. "It's as if you're trying to repel boys. When we got to choose a language last year, you could have picked French, the language of love. Instead, you had to choose German, the most masculine language on the face of the earth. Honestly, Steph, a girl taking German might as well write 'Gay and Proud' on her forehead."

"I don't believe it."

"Have you ever been asked out?"

I had no reply to toss back at her.

"And then there's your name."

"And what's wrong with *that*?"

"Nothing," said Alexandra. "If you'd use it. 'Stephanie' says slinky and shapely. A perfect name to go with long hair. But when I hear 'Steph,' the first thing that comes to my mind is 'strep.' As in 'strep throat.' I'm being brutally honest with you."

"Thanks. I noticed." I jammed my gloves in my pockets. "Of course, since I'm not slinky or shapely, and in fact am puny in every department, with freckles and oily, drab, brown hair, 'Steph' seems like the perfect name for me."

Alexandra was silent. She seemed to shrink into her parka, trying to be less tall, less blond, less beautiful. She kicked a rock.

"I'm sorry, Steph. Please delete this entire conversation." She mimed pressing a computer key. "You're incredibly intelligent, funny, loyal, another Marie Curie in our midst, and any bonehead boy who doesn't see this is a total idiot." We passed by the McQuillens' house. "Fortunately, the method we'll be using should attract a male who's worthy of you."

We could now glimpse the bay in the gaps between the spruces. We turned off the road toward an abandoned house.

"What about the 'Keep Out' sign?"

"You mustn't take everything so literally, Steph." She blazed a path down the unplowed drive, punching her boots through the foot of snow. "And despite my praise for your intelligence, it would be best to leave your literal, logical mind behind at this point."

"Hey, no problem. Call me Lucille Ball."

Gulls squawked mockingly above. We passed the empty house, its white paint peeling and half its windows boarded up. We tramped between a clothesline and a shed leaning drunkenly to one side. The water was in full view now, an icy wind plucking at it and turning my face to stone.

"So why are we here, of all places?"

"That's why." Alexandra stopped and pointed at a strange contraption near the edge of the cliff.

"What is it?"

We approached. It was as big as a box kite and mounted on a pole, gesticulating wildly with moving arms, vanes, wheels, and propellers large and small. I'd never seen it. It was all different colors. It didn't resemble anything in particular, except at the top, where there was a woman's head. Attached to her hair were three reflectors. Shells and chimes hung around her neck. Even with half the moving parts stuck, a gust blowing through it set off a flurry of fluttering and shimmering and ringing, as if a flock of exotic birds was taking flight.

I squinted my eyes against the wind. "Who made it?"

"I think we can rule out the Pilgrims. How should I know? It's always been here."

"What's written on the wood?"

" 'Lea Rosalia Santos Zamora.' "

"What's that?"

"I'm pretty sure it's a prayer to the wind."

"And how is this thing going to get me a boyfriend?"

"It isn't." Alexandra pulled a paperback book from her back pocket. "But this will."

She handed it to me. It was called *Guided Imagery*

for Successful Living. I gawked at her. "You've got to be kidding."

"Do you even know what guided imagery is?"

"No, but I know I don't like it."

"You said the same thing last year about boiling down Pepsi and pouring it over ice cream. Now you love it."

"This is different."

"Then you can forget what I said about Marie Curie. She *believed* in the scientific method. Observation, hypothesis, *experiment*—"

"So what's the hypothesis?"

"That thoughts are powerful. That they're the seeds of events. That by thinking something, we can help make it happen."

It was my turn to roll my eyes. "I can't believe you found a way to link Marie Curie with this mumbo jumbo."

"This is *not* mumbo jumbo." She took back the book and struggled to turn the pages with down mittens on her hands. "Here. Listen. 'All that is, is the result of what we have thought.' "

"Wow. I'm convinced. I want to join your cult. Unless we have to pierce our noses."

"That was written, for your information, by an ancient Buddhist monk."

"Named Yogi Berra."

"*Stop it*, Steph! This is serious!"

"I'll say it is, if I get frostbite standing here. Why can't we talk this over somewhere else?"

"Because this is the perfect place for guided imagery." She pointed at the flashing whirligig. "You can't see the wind, but look what it can do. It's invisible but powerful. Like thoughts. One brings a bunch of junk to life. The other brings desires to life. And it's better if you broadcast your thoughts outside. I did a visualization in this exact spot about acing an algebra test, and it worked. I'm sure it's because of the whirligig. It symbolizes all unseen forces." She stared at me. "It's like electricity—an invisible power that people didn't know existed for centuries. If you learn to use thoughts, you can do all kinds of things." She flipped through the book. "There are visualizations here to make you resistant to illness. To overcome stress. To build confidence."

"Let's hear it."

Alexandra stamped down a circle of snow and sat. I did the same, leaning my back against hers.

" 'Seek out a comfortable, nurturing place. Feel the gentle air against your skin.' "

"And your butt freezing to the ground."

" 'Perhaps you'll choose a quiet room or a peaceful corner of a garden. Breathe deeply. Feel yourself relax. Now feel the inner strength within you. Imagine this strength is a mighty river.' "

"Or for those with low confidence, a drip from a faucet."

" 'We're going to take a journey down this river.' "

"But remember—*do not drink the water*."

She threw down the book. "I'm trying to help you!" She dumped a handful of snow on my head. "But your scoffing, scientific mind won't let me. Secretly, you *want* to be an old maid. 'Despite her seven Nobel Prizes, the eighty-eight-year-old spinster was in contact with neither friends nor relations. Her decomposed body had apparently been lying on her laboratory floor for years. The corpse was identified through dental records.'"

"Now there's some imagery I could go for. *Seven* Nobel Prizes!"

"Laugh your head off."

"Listen, Alexandra. I'm sorry. But it's too much like those men on TV who bend spoons with their thoughts."

"That's quackery. This isn't."

"And are you going to tell me there's a fantasy in the book that attracts boyfriends?"

"Not exactly. I thought I'd create one just for you. You don't need a book. Anyone can lead a visualization."

"It's too cold and windy."

"The wind *helps*, don't you get it? It'll carry my words away like seeds and plant them in the future."

"You are a true mush-headed dreamer."

"Thank you. And you're a closed-minded skeptic. Now what do you say?"

"Either I say yes or I freeze to death arguing. Make it fast and let's go."

"Great!" she said. "But you wouldn't want me to skimp on details, would you? I mean, we're deciding your future here. You don't want the standard L.L. Bean WASP boyfriend, in plaid or navy. You want someone designed just for you."

"It's you I'm doing this for, not me."

"Have faith, *mon amie*. Okay. Close your eyes."

We were back to back, so she couldn't see me. I obeyed anyway.

"It's summer. July."

"Must be a cold spell."

"You feel the balmy air on your skin as you complete your pleasant morning's sail and tack into Portland's harbor. Your hand is on the tiller of the sixteen-foot, all-wood, gaff-rigged sailboat your parents have bought you. Painted across the stern is the name you've chosen for it—*Free Spirit*."

"Why not *Hunk o' Love* and my phone number?"

"*Shh! You'll wreck it!* You tie up at the dock. You haul down the sails and check the specimens in the holding tanks you've fitted it out with. You step ashore, your waist-length hair waving in the breeze like kelp."

"Guys really go for kelplike hair."

"Would you shut up and listen for a change!" She paused, seeming to search for what to have happen next.

"Leisurely, you make your way up to Belk's department store. You enter and glance at the perfumes, then know that the confidence and beauty you project is more potent than any scent. You go up two floors and try on a gorgeously embroidered French sundress. It is not on sale.

You buy it anyway and decide to wear it. Next, you drift into the lingerie department. You approach the bras, find the 28s, and don't stop until you reach the D cups."

"No!" I said. "That's *too* big!" I opened my eyes to see if the wind had already carried off this request. The whirligig was spinning merrily.

"You buy one. The scrawny saleswoman gives you an envious glare. Then you exit the store, stroll three doors down the block, and enter a coffeehouse. Your parents have encouraged you to drink coffee to slow your amazing growth—in this year, you've shot up to five-eight-and-a-half. Standing in line, you feel male eyes upon you. You turn and see him. He's tall, like you. His neck is as thick as a tree trunk. He glances back at his *Sports Illustrated*. His lips move not only when he reads, but when he looks at the photographs. A Neanderthal. You avert your eyes. You get an iced coffee and take a seat far away."

"My teeth are chattering like maniacs and I'm supposed to imagine drinking iced coffee?"

"Quiet! You pick up a French newspaper from an empty table and begin to read. Fluently. Through an intensive course on videotape, you've mastered the language in record time. Last night, you realize, you had a dream in French—powerfully erotic, drenching you in sweat. A man now approaches." She paused, deliberating. "He's wearing a beret. He's handsome, young, and speaks to you in French. You instantly detect his faulty pronunciation of the French *r*. Then an incorrect participle. He's a coffeehouse cad, a pickup artist. You send him away with a brisk *'Laissez-moi!'*"

"An idiom meaning 'I'm not real anyway.'"

"You finish your drink, walk to a bookstore, and wander over to the magazines. You pick up the latest *Crab and Clam*. Reading it while sauntering down the sidewalk, you feel a nudge. A man's grabbing your purse! Your body is ready, fluid, and forceful as you crush his instep and try out a new combination of moves from your self-defense training. You regret that he'll be in traction for years. The police cart him off and compliment you. You're discouraged, however, by the sad specimens of manhood you've encountered this day. The glow of your mental and physical powers is a beacon, alas, to the entire male sex."

"Aren't you getting a little grabby?"

She was silent. Then she inhaled deeply, as if swelling with inspiration.

"You walk back to your boat and examine more closely the strange eel you netted on the way down. You suspect you've discovered a new species and wonder who you'll name it for, immortalizing the person you choose. You raise the sails, cast off, and head out." She paused. "Past Princes Point you spot something to starboard. A lobster buoy? No—a human head. Then a hand comes up, waving for help. You tack, come alongside, heave to, and help the unfortunate aboard. He's sixteen, tall and lean, with a Gypsy's black hair and soulful eyes. He can't stop shivering."

"There's something we have in common."

"He'd capsized while sea kayaking and had become separated from his craft. You help him take off his wet clothes and wrap him in a blanket. He's unable to get warm. You spot the symptoms of hypothermia. You have no hot drinks or source of heat. Suddenly, from your first-aid class, you remember about heat donation. Without a thought, you do as you'd learned. You throw off your sundress and everything underneath and embrace him tightly under the blanket, passing your body's warmth to his."

She halted, seeming to savor the story. "The color begins to return to his cheeks. You notice the slightest of accents when he speaks. He reveals that he's Canadian— French-Canadian. He spots your copy of *Crab and Clam* and mentions that he has a subscription. For five years he's been studying barnacle reproduction. Sadness clouds his eyes when he tells you that both of his parents are dead and that barnacles are his only real family. You remain together under the blanket longer than is strictly required." She paused. "When you emerge, he knows there will be more in his life than barnacles. And you— you know who you'll name your new species for."

Alexandra was quiet for a time. "Now just sit, eyes closed, and hold the image in your head."

"Like a—"

"With your sarcastic mouth shut."

I leaned back against her for five frigid minutes, listening to the invisible wind powering the whirligig. It rattled, hummed, squeaked, and chimed. Then I heard a different kind of sound. A human sound. A soft throat-clearing. I opened my eyes. My heart began racing. Had her words lured a mate already? Impossible, I thought. I was still five-foot-one. But what else would bring someone to the point in that weather?

Disbelieving, fearful, hopeful, I slowly turned my head and stared.

All that was three winters ago. I'm only five-foot-four. Still a 28-A. I do not own my own sailboat. I still classify my manner of thinking as logical and scientific. Which is why I have trouble explaining how the nine-year-old boy who watched us that day turned out to be the little brother of Kyle, who lives two towns west and was visiting relatives here over Christmas—the McQuillens. And who's been my heart's joy since that day we met. He is neither French, French-Canadian, tall, a biologist, nor a sea kayaker. Jazz trumpet is his life. He plays his compositions to me over the phone.

I haven't become a mush-headed dreamer. But just in case unseen forces do exist, I pay my respects to them by keeping the whirligig painted and repaired. I check it after every winter. Sometimes Alexandra helps. We're careful about what we say while we're there. Despite which, I had no hesitation in announcing that when I discover a new species, out of gratitude I'll give it her name.

The Afterlife

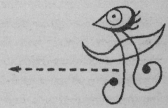

The day's first squirt of sunlight hit the window. The bus changed gears. Brent opened his eyes. They were climbing through mountains now. The other passengers around him were sleeping. Twitched alert by the light, he craned his neck to get a better view, pressed his head to the tinted glass, and raptly observed the sun's rising. After night came another day. And after death another life. Mornings seemed mysterious gifts. He inspected the dawn with fascination.

The bus's gears growled. Behind him he heard a faint conversation in another language. This is the afterlife, he told himself. To be crowded in with a collection of strangers, plunging through a foreign landscape, headed toward an unknown destiny. The bus was his ferry across the river Styx. It descended now into an unlit valley. Brent squinted at his map and realized he was in the Cascades. Seattle wasn't far off. He'd been riding for two days, watching new souls board in Milwaukee, Minneapolis, Fargo, Bozeman, Butte, Coeur d'Alene, Spokane. He'd speculated on their previous lives. He had surprisingly little interest in his own. His second life had eclipsed his first. Its moment of birth had been the crash.

He didn't remember the actual impact. He did recall the ambulance lights, the policeman asking how he felt, the discovery that he'd escaped with only cuts and a minor head injury. Then came the alcohol test. Then the drive to the police station, being booked for drunk driving, the photographs and fingerprints—registering his new birth, he thought now. Then the realization that the ambulance at the scene had been tending someone else, that he'd hit another car. His father had arrived at the station. There was talk of the Chevy, its back end mangled, the car probably totaled. Then the news, delivered by one of the officers, that the woman he'd hit had died.

The muteness had begun in that moment. He spoke not at all driving home with his father, slept fourteen hours, and didn't speak the next day. He remembered the party and that he'd tried to kill himself. That he'd ended up killing someone else left him frozen, numb from scalp to soles. Words returned on the second day. His turmoil, though, wasn't translatable into words.

His mother got rid of the newspaper that had a story

about the crash, but Brent dug it out of the bottom of the trash can. His car had apparently hit the divider, spun, then been struck by the driver behind him. His blood alcohol was .11. The story was brief and gave only the victim's name, age, and residence: Lea Zamora, 18, Chicago. He plumbed those few facts. She was nearly his own age. He was determined to know more. He tried the obituaries, but her name wasn't listed. He rummaged through the trash for the following day's paper, turned to the gravy-stained obituaries—and found her. Daughter of Cesar and Tamara Zamora, senior at Niles North High School, an honor student, member of the student council, the orchestra, the track team, active in the Filipino community, volunteer at Resurrection Hospital. Why did he have to kill someone like that? Then he realized with a surge of relief that he could perhaps go to the funeral. The police had confiscated his license, but he could take a cab, stand in the back, leave an anonymous offering of some kind. He checked the paper. It had been held the day before.

He ate little, spoke little, and no longer listened to music. He turned seventeen, an event he scarcely noticed. He heard his parents whisper about the blow to his head and his personality change. He'd been diagnosed with a mild concussion. The headaches, like a wrecking ball working on his skull, came less often, replaced by the endless tolling in his mind of the word *murderer*. Everyone knew. He refused to go to school and made arrangements to finish his classwork at home. He disliked being seen in his neighborhood, where the glances he drew were too long or too short. Among strangers he felt no less an outcast, their blind assumption that he was one of them making him wince inside. He studied their carefree innocence with envy: an old woman reading on a bench in a mall, a baby sleeping in a stroller, a pretzel seller joking with a customer. He was no longer of their kind and never would be.

There was a hearing with a judge soon after the crash. Like a ghost, Brent listened to other people discuss the accident and his fate. He was charged with DUI and manslaughter. He hadn't contested his guilt; his punishment was the issue at hand. The judge asked for more information and set a date for a second hearing. It was then that the interviewing began. Social workers and psychologists questioned him, his parents, his friends. He found the fact that he'd tried to kill himself impossible to share with another soul. He could scarcely believe he'd actually tried it and wondered how he could have given no thought to the other cars he would hit. His parents hired their own lawyer and a psychologist. Their job was to argue that sending him to the juvenile detention center would be detrimental to his worrisome mental state. His father tried to cheer him up, promising he would serve no time, telling him to put it behind him, assuring him people would forget.

"I won't," Brent answered silently. He took the obituary from its hiding place, looked up Cesar Zamora in the phone book, and spent all of one day composing what became a four-sentence apology. He mailed it on a Monday. The reply came on Friday—an envelope with his own letter inside, mutilated with scissors, stabbed, defaced with cigarette burns.

Nightmares about Mr. Zamora stalking him through the Philippine jungle joined those about the detention center. Entering the courthouse for his second hearing, the latest dream of being beaten by a circle of inmates recurred to him. He passed a young man, his arms swarming with tattoos, whom he was certain he'd seen in the dream. He and his parents found their room. The psychologists spoke, then the lawyers. Brent suddenly wondered if Mr. Zamora might be there. He was trying to scan the faces to his rear when his father squeezed his forearm. The judge was addressing him, sentencing him to probation in place of the detention center. His parents beamed. He felt relief, but also an unanswered hunger. He realized he wanted a punishment. Brent knew also that, grim as the detention center might be, he'd have welcomed the chance to leave his family and his previous life behind. The listing of the terms of his probation hardly registered with him—alcohol counseling, therapy for depression, volunteering in an emergency room. Then the judge came to the final item: meeting with the victim's family, if they desired, to discuss restitution.

Brent knew the meeting would never take place, an

outcome that once again left him both relieved and unsatisfied. He wanted to do something for the family. Two days later the probation officer called. The victim's mother had agreed to talk with him.

The meeting was scheduled in a building downtown. Entering, Brent wished his parents weren't with him. The room was spacious and had a view of Lake Michigan. Miss Gill, young and black and soft-voiced, was there to serve as mediator. A few minutes later Mrs. Zamora arrived, not the tiny Asian woman Brent had pictured but a heavyset redhead in an India print skirt. Among the dozen necklaces jangling on her chest, Brent picked out pendants of an astrological sign and a Native American sun symbol. Her wavy hair flowed exuberantly over her shoulders; the rest of her seemed only half-alive. She navigated the introductions with an eerie, ethereal calm. Brent gazed openly into her face, offering himself up to her, and noticed that her eyes were slightly bloodshot. Those eyes searched his own, then released him. How strange, he thought, that he'd somehow caused this woman, whom he'd never met, to cry.

"We're meeting today," said Miss Gill, "to apologize, and to understand, and to atone." Her voice was hopeful rather than accusing. "We never know all the consequences of our acts. They reach into places we can't see. And into the future, where no one can."

She looked at Brent, then invited Mrs. Zamora to describe the results of Lea's death.

"When the phone rang," she began, "I was sorting through lentils, to soak for soup the next day." Her voice had a faint flutter to it. Eyes down, she continued her detailed, dispassionate account of that night and the days that followed, of her husband's smashing a wooden chair in his rage, the younger children's endless crying, her sleeplessness, the thought of killing herself to be with Lea, the voice from Lea's photo saying, "No."

Brent closed his eyes. What murderous machine had he constructed and set in motion? When his turn finally came to speak, the long apology he'd rehearsed reduced itself to the two words "I'm sorry," words he spoke over and over, then wailed miserably through tears, not caring that his parents were watching.

Miss Gill spoke for a while. When it came time to discuss restitution, Brent saw his father shift nervously. The Zamoras hadn't sued; apparently they were content with the insurance company's payment. His father had brought his checkbook just in case. Brent spied the silver pen beside it in his jacket's inside pocket, stationed like a butler awaiting command. Miss Gill reviewed various possibilities: a written apology to each family member, service to a charity of the Zamoras' choice, service to the Zamoras themselves. Whatever it might be would have to be agreeable to both parties.

Mrs. Zamora stared back at her. "I don't believe in retribution. Lea was born in the Philippines. I was teaching English and met my husband there. I saw what an-eye-for-an-eye looks like, with the rebels fighting the government and all that. My husband feels a little differently. I also believe everything happens for a reason." She toyed with her necklaces. "That the universe required this. For some reason."

She paused, then directed her words at Brent's parents. "Lea had a very caring soul. Very strong and generous. Everybody who saw her smiled. They loved her at the hospital where she worked. This summer she was going to do volunteer work in California. In the fall, she was going to college in Boston. She would have spread joy all over the country."

Brent wondered what his own eulogy would sound like. Mrs. Zamora turned her gaze on him.

"I've thought about you, for hours and hours. What can you possibly do for me? Paint the house? Mow the lawn all summer?"

Her voice had acquired a stronger tremble. She let the questions hang in the air, then looked to Brent's left, out the window.

"My father is a very fine carpenter. Lea was his first grandchild. When she was little, he made her lots of wooden toys. Her favorite was a whirligig, of a girl with arms that spin in the wind. He painted the face to look like her. We've had it on a pole in our yard forever. Hundreds of people over the years have noticed it, and stopped, and smiled. Just like people smiled at Lea."

She opened her purse, extracted a photo, looked at it, and passed it to Brent. It showed the wind toy in motion.

"Lea is gone. I'm learning to accept that. I thought I had nothing I could ask you that would help. You can't bring back her body. Then I thought about her spirit."

Brent's skin tingled. He stared at the photo, then at her, anxious to hear her bidding.

"This is my only request. That you make four whirligigs, of a girl that looks like Lea. Put her name on them. Then set them up in Washington, California, Florida, and Maine—the corners of the United States. Let people all over the country receive joy from her even though she's gone. You make the smiles that she would have made. It's the only thing you can do for me." She exhaled. "That's what I ask."

"You must be joking," said Brent's mother.

His father strained forward in his chair. "This is crazy!" He appealed to Miss Gill. "That's not the kind of thing you ask for!" He faced Mrs. Zamora. "And how's he supposed to zip around the country? In his private jet?"

She pulled something else out of her purse. "I bought him a Greyhound bus pass. Good for forty-five days. He can go anywhere."

Miss Gill repeated that restitutions weren't imposed, but accepted voluntarily by the offender. Brent's parents raised one objection after another, from his commitment to the emergency room to his need for his family, his nonexistent carpentry skills, and the cruel and unusual conditions of bus travel. Brent was oblivious of the arguing. In the quiet storm cellar of his mind, he pondered the proposal. Strange as it was, it would get him away from Chicago, his parents, and his recent past. It would also give him a chance to do penance. He'd never traveled on his own before. The idea held sudden appeal. He smiled inside. He cleared his throat. Then he spoke the words, "I'll do it."

The bus sped down the Cascades like a skier. Then the road flattened. Brent saw a man point. He turned and beheld a peak in the distance that seemed a mirage, impossibly high, snow shimmering on its wide shoulders, the absolute lord of the landscape. The word *Rainier* passed down the aisle. Brent gawked. It seemed too large, as a full moon does when it first rises into view. He'd never been west of Chicago before. He was sure he was there now.

He opened his whirligig book and looked through it between glances out the window. He'd found it in the sixth store he'd tried, a dingy used book shop downtown on Wabash Avenue. It was an old, loose-spined hardback called *Make Your Own Whirligigs and Weathervanes*. A previous owner had penciled tiny, masculine-looking notes in the margins. Brent wondered where the man was at that moment and tried to imagine him from his handwriting. He saw a balding head and glasses. Strange, he thought, that they would never recognize each other if they met.

He flipped ahead to a whirligig of a man milking a cow. He'd read only the chapter on supplies. He knew he should have tried building one in Chicago, but he hadn't. Once his probation officer had convinced Brent's parents that the trip might help him, he'd been in a rush to leave. He eyed his blue backpacker's pack on the rack and felt separate from all the other passengers. Their luggage held shirts and pants; his held slabs of plywood, a saw, a hand drill, dowels, brass rods, pliers, a quart of varnish, nails, paints. He watched his pack closely, dreading his tools spilling out. He'd probably be accused of making bombs. He imagined replying with the truth, that he was a builder of whirligigs. Why not? No one knew anything about him. Here was a chance not simply to alter his past, as he'd done in school, but to actually live a different life. He tried out the words in his head: "I'm a traveling whirligig maker." It was an interim identity, tied to his previous life. He would cast it off soon, but in favor of what? He was lodged in his own chrysalis but had no idea what he was turning into.

They passed through Preston, then Issaquah. The old man next to Brent was still sleeping. In twenty-four hours they hadn't exchanged ten words. He observed two women in front of him exclaiming over wallet photos and marveled at how naturally some people spun lines of connection, turning a world of strangers into family.

He opened his own wallet, took out Lea's picture, and studied it in solitude. He found her entrancing. She looked Hawaiian, her skin the color of cinnamon, smooth as sanded wood, her forehead high, her hair long and straight. Her eyes were faintly Asian. He probed the photo for new information and now saw that she'd drawn her hair, shiny and black as obsidian, to the side with a clip. Her dress was white. Or was it only a blouse? He examined the pattern embroidered on the bodice. She wore a gold necklace, fine as spider's silk, but he couldn't see what hung from it. He scrutinized her smile from close range, almost felt her breath on his face. Strange to think she was now smiling at her killer. Yet she wasn't— her head was turned at an angle. He stared into her cheerful brown eyes, knowing she would never look back at him but always off to the side. This was a relief. Her direct gaze would have vaporized him with accusation.

He turned the photo over and read her full name, Lea Rosalia Santos Zamora, written in her mother's curlicued script. She'd given him the picture as a model for the whirligigs, along with a disposable camera. Strangely, she wanted photos of them but didn't want to know their locations. The idea of coming upon one, she'd told him, rusted or vandalized or fallen over, lifeless like her daughter, was too forbidding. She preferred to see them in her mind, where they could spin forever, safe from all harm.

Suburbs appeared out the window. Then the bus nosed its way through a long tunnel and emerged into downtown Seattle. The streets were hilly. Brent glimpsed Puget Sound. He wanted a longer view, but the bus turned, following its usual labyrinthine path to the station. He glanced at his United States map. Interstate 90 ended here, the same road that led all the way back to Chicago, that passed a few miles from his house. He felt himself a departing sailor, leaving the sight of land behind. The bus found the station. The brakes sighed. He grabbed his pack and climbed down.

His voice sounded odd in his ears when he asked for directions to the water. He tightened down his sleeping bag, struggled into his pack, and set off, staggering like a grizzly walking upright. It was early in July and sunny. He sampled the air, amazed at how light it felt, so different from the weighted, humid heat he was used to. He followed bustling Stewart Street, viewing the cars and pedestrians curiously. How like the afterlife it all was: a populous city, reached only after a long journey toward the setting sun, here all along but never seen until now. Was Lea here somewhere? Walking on, he jerked at the sight of a face vaguely resembling hers, then arrived at tourist-thronged Pike Place Market. He passed up the chance for a squidburger, bought two hot dogs instead, and watched a juggler while he ate. The crowds bothered him. It felt more like Chicago than the pristine Pacific Northwest he'd heard of. He left, following signs to Waterfront Park. This turned out to be piers and amusements. He looked over the water. A line of blue mountains floated above the clouds in the distance. That was the Washington he wanted. Lea's mother hadn't specified where in the four states he should put the whirligigs. He bought a map and some groceries, walked back to the station, and took the next bus north.

He got off in Mount Vernon and pored over his map. He broke his promise to his parents not to hitchhike, found a ride with a fisherman heading west, then walked three miles to a state park on the water only to find that the campground was full. He hadn't realized it was Fourth of July weekend. Seeing that he'd walked, the ranger suggested he try asking if he could share a site. Slowly, Brent meandered through the campground. Every site was a separate country, baseball blaring from a radio in one while the next was occupied by a couple playing duets on soprano recorders. It struck him that every family was a universe, with its own peculiar natural laws. Free of his own family, he imagined himself part of each one he passed, trying on identities like a quick-change artist. He neared the end of the campground. He paused, stealthily eyeing a bearded man unloading his tent from a bicycle. He was tall, fit, looked to be in his thirties, had a thoughtful, sunburned face. The man noticed him, stopped, and turned. Brent felt like a stray dog begging scraps.

"I was wondering . . ." His voice was rusted from disuse. He cleared his throat. "If you'd mind . . ."

"If you picked out a corner for yourself? Be my guest."

"I'll pay half the fee," Brent added quickly.

"No need. Glad to have the company."

The site was on the water and more private than most. Brent was pleased. He took off his pack, pried off his sneakers, waded in up to his calves, and washed his face in Puget Sound.

It was too late to begin on the whirligig. He pulled out his tent, an open tube of plastic meant to hang from a rope strung between two trees. He'd been sent to a camp for a week a few times, but not lately, and had never camped out on his own. He stood with his rope, unable to find flat ground furnished with properly spaced trees. He hoped the cyclist wasn't watching him and saw the man's dome tent suddenly spring up like a magician's illusion. Brent scanned the sky. It didn't look like rain. He put the tent back and unrolled his sleeping bag.

"And what brings you here?" the cyclist asked over dinner.

They'd collaborated on the fire. Brent stirred his pan of beef and barley soup. "Just seeing the country," he answered offhandedly. "What about you?"

"Riding south from Canada. Heading down the coast to San Francisco. Seeing the country, like yourself. Studying the strange customs of the natives. No offense meant."

"Where are you from?"

"Prince George, British Columbia. Halfway up toward the Yukon."

The name raised visions of the far north in Brent's mind. He'd never met a Canadian before and felt like an explorer who's just heard tell of an unknown continent.

"Ever play Go?" the man asked. "The game."

"Never heard of it."

"Like to learn?"

After dinner the cyclist produced a folding board and two tiny boxes of stones, black and white. "It's from China originally, like most things. I'm still learning myself. Brought a book about it, to study on the trip." He gave Brent the white stones, shaped like flying saucers, polished and identical. "Supposed to be excellent training for generals. Some say it won the Vietnam War for the North. Wheaties for the brain."

He explained the rules and they began a practice game. The object was to secure territory, arranging groups of stones into living communities that couldn't be extinguished by your opponent. Brent felt he was practicing constructing his new life. Out of nowhere, the word *karass* came to mind, from the Vonnegut book he'd read in English, a term for a disparate group of people linked together without their knowledge. Your family and friends weren't part of your *karass*. You couldn't choose its members, and might never know who was in it or what its purpose was. Brent felt certain that Lea was a member of his. Was the cyclist part of it too?

Sunset flared orange on the water. Firecrackers began going off.

"Ah, yes," said the man. "Noisemaking devices to dispel evil spirits on this important day."

Brent couldn't reveal why he shared the same distanced perspective. This second time around, he saw everything from the outside. Much that he'd taken for granted before now struck him as curious: handshaking, the Pledge of Allegiance, neckties on men, sports teams named for animals . . .

The sky shifted to shades from the spectrum's outer edges, then went black. The cyclist lit a tiny gas lamp that hissed and glowed like a shard from a star. By its light they played another hour, then retired. Brent climbed into his sleeping bag. Radios, firecrackers, voices subsided, replaced by the chirring of crickets, a breeze's passage through the trees, the waves' steady respiration. The nonhuman world was emerging, a world he'd rarely noticed, another hidden city. Was Lea now a citizen here? He wondered if the creature he heard creeping over dry leaves could be her. He imagined her fully fluent here, able to hear and comprehend what he couldn't, her sense of smell greatly magnified, this bit of shoreline known to her as it never would be to him. He looked up at the stars, glinting silently, a movie without a soundtrack. Or was he simply deaf to their music? He realized he knew no constellations. Likewise the names of trees, flowers, rocks, birds, insects, fish. He was a foreigner here. He wished he knew some names.

When he awoke, the cyclist was just leaving. It was

cold. Brent's bag was damp with dew. Huddling within, waiting for the sun to top the trees and warm the world, he understood why people had worshiped it. Two hours later he'd taken a shower, breakfasted on French bread and cheese, skimmed three chapters of the whirligig book, and picked the simplest project offered—an angel whose spinning arms played a harp.

He studied the diagrams apprehensively. Neither he nor his father was the *Popular Mechanics* type. There were practically no tools in his house; those he'd brought with him had all been bought new. It had been four years since he'd taken woodshop, where he'd spent weeks on a simple hinged-top box. Maybe he'd changed in that time. He felt Lea and Mrs. Zamora watching him, and hoped that he had.

He walked to his pack. He'd brought four pieces of plywood, one foot by two feet, marine grade, half an inch thick. He drew one out, sat at the table, and sketched the angel's outline on it, then erased it all. Freehand drawing was not his forte either. It took half an hour to get it right. He tightened the wood down to the table with a clamp, started in with his D-shaped coping saw, and promptly broke the thin blade. He inserted the only spare he'd brought, feeling like a soldier down to his last bullet. He worked gingerly. The blade survived. The file that followed the same path not only smoothed the wood's edge but snapped off a sizable chunk of the angel's wing. He slammed the file onto the table. He hated wood. He took a break, frightened by his anger in the face of this setback. There was no channel-changer here. He picked up the whirligig book and stared at the previous owner's patient, precise script. He almost felt the man was with him, telling him to settle down and conquer the project calmly, step by step.

He sat down. He decided to do without the wing. The figure could simply be a harp player. The harp was full-sized, the sort you'd find in an orchestra. Lea had played in an orchestra. He wondered what her instrument was. He sawed off the rest of the wing, sanded the wood, then went to his pack and dug out his five tubes of acrylic paint. In the trash can he found a styrofoam cup, which he filled with water for cleaning his brushes. From the same source he retrieved a paper plate to use as a palette. He painted one side of the figure, let it dry a bit, then leaned it on a stone and painted the other, making her hair black rather than the yellow prescribed by the book. Down one side he printed Lea's name with a black permanent marker, then used it and his tape measure to draw the harp strings. He considered his work. It wasn't perfect, especially the outline of the face. It looked nothing like her picture. He repainted the mouth, but only made matters worse. The two sides should have been identical, but weren't. It was the best he could do. He stopped and ate lunch.

All afternoon was spent on Lea's propeller-shaped arms. He'd begun referring to the whirligig by her name and almost felt he was reassembling her broken body, reviving her. Each arm required much whittling and sanding. Suddenly he was halted by the strangeness of his task. He saw it as his parents had. "Why am I doing this?" he said aloud. The whole enterprise seemed taken from a dream, incomprehensible in the light of day.

He returned to work. What he knew without question was that it felt good to be busy toiling in atonement, to direct his feelings outward through his arms and knife, as if draining an abscess. Now and then his eyes crossed Puget Sound to the Olympic range and settled on the peak the cyclist had told him was Mount Olympus. The home of the Greek gods, Brent mused. Hadn't Hercules likewise performed his labors to cleanse himself of a crime? From Miss Lifton's class, in his previous life, the story returned to him while he worked, of the Greek hero slaying his wife and children in a fit of insanity, his asking an oracle how he could atone, her telling him to seek out a certain king and perform for him twelve labors. His tasks had been just as bizarre as Brent's and likewise had called for long journeys.

Brent worked until late. He cut his hand three different times and suspected that part of him wasn't content with the labors he'd been assigned and longed to mete out more punishment. He laid out the whirligig's various parts and set them shining with a thick coat of varnish. Lea's eyes glistened as if she'd awakened. Finally, he put down his tools, built a fire, and warmed another can of soup.

He returned to work early the next morning. Bent over his book like a biblical scholar, mumbling, rereading, receiving sudden insights, he carefully mounted the arms on the figure. The placement was tricky. He tried to figure out why one arm didn't spin and adjusted it endlessly. Next he agonized over the figure's pivot point, marked the spot, drilled the hole, and hoped for the best. He pounded some tubing into the hole. He slipped this over a piece of dowel. The figure turned smoothly from side to side. He glued the dowel into a chunk of two-by-four he found along the shore. He tingled. He realized he was finished. He blew upon it. The arms pinwheeled, seeming to strum the harp strings. He could hardly believe it actually worked. He blew fifty more times for confirmation.

He now wondered where to set it up. Was it illegal to mount it on state land? Then again, the park belonged to the public. Better here than in someone's front yard. He'd have to hope the harpist so charmed the rangers that they wouldn't remove it. How to mount it was a further problem. He hadn't brought ten-foot poles in his pack. He paced the site, deliberating. Then he spied a tree limb, roughly horizontal, open to the wind from the west and high enough to keep his work out of reach. He climbed out and nailed down the driftwood mount. Then he returned for the whirligig.

Back on the ground, he stared up at it. The harp player was just over a foot tall and seemed much smaller from a distance. Brent awaited a breeze until his neck ached. When it came, the figure felt it first. It swung on the dowel like a weathervane. The arms lifted, then trembled. Then spun. He felt the breeze. The arms gained speed. His smile widened. The phrase "the breath of life" traveled through his mind. He watched, mesmerized. Then he ran for the camera.

Miami, Florida

Still dark outside. No traffic. Just me. This is how I like it. *Muy tranquilo.*

I never saw a street-sweeper machine in my life until I came from Puerto Rico. The first week here, it woke me up. I was eleven. I thought it was a monster. Then I looked out the window and saw it pass. I saw the man inside. I wondered what he thinks about, driving all night in the dark, alone. And now *I'm* driving a street-sweeper. Maybe the same one. And now I know what the driver thinks. Watching the curb. Watching parked cars. Looking down at the gutter broom. Thinking when to use the sprayer. Thinking about other times in my life. Enjoying the peaceful night.

Peace is a very hard thing to find. The Pope is always

asking for peace. He tells all the countries to stop their wars. Every year he tells them, but more wars always come. Always people disagree and fight.

I think about why this is while I drive. I think about the shearwater bird.

It's March. Still cool at night. Like Puerto Rico, in the mountains, where I lived. The air was cool there. Life was more calm. For a while, anyway. Then my father had to sell our farm to a power company. Lots of families had to. They covered our farm with water to make a lake, to make electricity. Many people there were angry. My family left the mountains, where we'd always lived.

We moved to San Juan, on the coast. San Juan is a very big city. There were five children in my family. People laughed at how we talked. Boys fought me. Some people laughed at my father's straw hat. Many times I heard my father and mother argue. Other people argued against the government. Some wanted Puerto Rico to join the United States. Others wanted it to be its own country. Others wanted it to be something else. All were fighting against each other. One day a bomb went off near our house. I ran to see. Then I wish I didn't. I saw a man lying down in his own blood. One month later we flew in a plane to Miami.

No one in my family spoke English. In the mountains there was only Spanish. In school here I listened to the teacher but I didn't understand anything. I would look a long time at her ring and her necklace and her shoes and at other students and out the window. That's all I did that first year. The next year I went to junior high. There was lots to look at in woodworking class. But my teacher got mad when I didn't look at him. He asked me a question one time. I didn't know what he said, so I didn't say anything back. His face got red. He ran up to my chair. Then he grabbed my hair and lifted me up and yelled some words right in my face. I hated that teacher. He didn't know Spanish. When he let me go I swore at him in Spanish. Then I ran out of the room and went home.

Next week, they made me take a test. Then they said I could move to a different school. I was glad. Then I went there. It was a school for retarded children. That's where they put kids who didn't know English. I told my father I wouldn't go. He said school in America makes your life better. We had lots of arguments. I pretended to go, but instead I would walk around or go to the park to watch the tennis players. When I was fourteen, I got a job in a restaurant when I was supposed to be in school. I brought home the money and gave it to my father. I knew he needed it, for the rent. He took it. I quit pretending to go to school after that.

In the restaurant I worked the dishwasher machine. Everyone spoke Spanish. I liked it there. The waitresses all called me Flaco because I was skinny. They used to bring me food. It was a good job. But people argued there too. There were two cooks. One from Puerto Rico. He only liked Puerto Rican salsa music. Willie Colón was his favorite. He brought in tapes of Willie Colón's band and would hit the spatula on the grill like a drum. The other cook was from Jamaica. He only liked reggae. On weekends, there was a third cook, from Cuba. They used to fight over the tape player. Not even the Pope could stop this war.

Four years I worked there. Then the restaurant closed. I got a job in a different restaurant. Many people spoke English there. I learned how to speak from them. Constancia was one of the waitresses. Eighteen years old, also from Puerto Rico. She was so beautiful that everyone gave her big tips. Some she would give to the dishwasher and busboys. She always gave more to me than to the others. We became engaged. Then we got married. That was a very happy time. We lived with her mother. Constancia was not only beautiful but very kind, very good. Every day I told myself that I was lucky.

I went to class at night to learn English better, to get a better job. English is very strange. You chop a tree *down*, then you chop it *up*. *Muy loco*. I filled out a form and got a job with the city, fixing holes in the street. Much more money than from the restaurant. We had a party to celebrate. At the party, Constancia announced that she was pregnant. Her mother, my mother, my father, everyone was very happy for us.

Down that street, to the right, at the red light, is the hospital where the baby was born. A very beautiful little girl. Everyone loved her very much. Constancia stopped work in the restaurant to stay home with the baby. She was a very good mother. When the baby was just one year old, it got a cold. This cold got worse. Then it went into the baby's lungs. It kept coughing and sweating. And then it died.

After this, Constancia changed. She didn't go back to work in the restaurant. She missed the baby very much. Instead of hearing the baby's voice, she turned on the TV and let it talk all day long. When she watched, her eyes didn't move. Her face was like one of the statues in church.

One year later, we had another baby. This time a boy. We named him Raul. This time Constancia was different. Instead of laughing and smiling at the baby, she was worried all the time. She was afraid he would get sick, like the first baby. Raul learned how to crawl and started putting everything in his mouth. Every day Constancia would mop the floor and vacuum the rug. She bought a special spray to kill germs. She sprayed it on his toys and the TV and the furniture. In summer, red dust falls on Miami. People say it's from the desert in Africa, that the wind blows it across the ocean. Constancia was afraid it would bring bad diseases. She went to a *botánica* and bought special candles and statues of saints and prayers to hang over Raul's crib.

When Raul was four Constancia's grandmother and grandfather came from Puerto Rico to live in our house. All day the grandfather played dominoes in our kitchen with the man next door and argued about politics. He also liked to watch soccer on TV. His hearing was bad, so the TV had to be loud. The grandmother was always telling Constancia how to take care of Raul. "Feed him more plantain, like in Puerto Rico. French fries are very bad for the stomach." We taught Raul English, but the grandparents didn't like this. We talked to him in English. They talked to him in Spanish. Constancia's mother tried to keep everything peaceful. Impossible. It was like a war in our house.

One night on TV I saw a picture of a bird flying over the ocean. The announcer said this bird lives almost all its life on the ocean. He said it was called a shearwater. I wished that I could be that bird. Live alone, far away from land. No other birds around. Very peaceful.

I had a cousin in New Jersey. He moved in with us. Seventeen years old. Constancia's mother wanted him to leave. He was always playing rock and roll on the radio. He stayed out at night, very late. I saved enough money for a car. The first time he drove it he had an accident. We had a big argument about it. Then I lost my job. All day I was home with Raul. I tried to play with him. Constancia wouldn't let him play in the street or even on the sidewalk. He couldn't ride in the car unless he wore a special charm around his neck. I looked for a job, but couldn't find anything. Our money got very low. Constancia started bringing in money by taking care of babies for women who worked. First it was two babies. Then three. Then five. There was always a baby crying. And the grandparents yelling. And the TV loud. And rock and roll loud. Everybody arguing. One morning, very early, before it was light, I got in the car and drove. Not driving to look for a job. Just driving.

I got out of Miami. Drove through the Everglades. Very peaceful. I rolled down the windows. It felt great. I drove two hours, across to the Gulf. I parked at a beach. I walked out, watched the waves. No one was there. A little breeze off the water. Very quiet. Very nice.

After a while I got hungry. I got back in the car and drove farther. I came to a town. I walked out on the pier. Nailed to the wall of a restaurant was a little marching band made of wood. An arrow under it pointed to the front door and said "March On In." I went in and ate breakfast. Then I walked to the end of the pier. It was still early and cool. I saw people getting on a fishing boat. Then I remembered the shearwater bird. I'd been thinking about it for months. They said you couldn't see it from land. You'd have to go on a boat. I asked the captain if he'd ever seen one. He said all the time. I told him I didn't want to fish. I only wanted to see a shearwater. He let me on for half price.

We left. Everyone else was busy getting their poles ready. Not me. I stood up at the front, looking for the bird. The captain would stop to let people fish, then start up again. I looked back. I couldn't see land. That felt good. I felt like a shearwater.

The sky was clear. The water was very calm. We went farther and farther. Then the captain called to me. He pointed. Following the boat was a flock of birds. Diving into the water. Fighting over fish. Stealing fish from each other. Very noisy. He said those were shearwaters.

I watched. I couldn't believe those were the birds I'd been dreaming of. They followed us a long way. I felt sad all the way back to land.

I got off the boat and walked down the pier. I came to that wooden marching band. I stopped and looked. There was a trumpet, trombone, clarinet, and drum. Birds don't live alone, I told myself. They live in flocks. Like people. People are always in a group. Like that little wooden band. And whenever there's a group, there's fighting. If the people in a group get along, maybe they make good music instead of arguing, like Willie Colón's band. But usually not. That's how life is. I stared at that marching band. Then I got in the car and drove home.

That was last year. In summer I got this job driving the street-sweeper. Two o'clock in the morning until ten. Very peaceful during the night. Then the sun comes up. The traffic starts, everyone's in a hurry, cars honk and go around me. All that will start in an hour. I'm ready for it. I always bring a tape player. I'll put on some music. Willie Colón's band.

Twinkle Twinkle
Little Star

The sun had long set. To the west, over the Pacific, the sky was still faintly blue, clinging to the memory of day. Brent moved to a seat across the aisle so as to scan the darker eastern sky, waited through a long stretch of trees, then thought he spotted it: Deneb, in the constellation Cygnus, the swan. He squinted at his book, then out the bus window. Now that they were out of Los Angeles, the air was much clearer. He looked again and was amazed to make out the shape of a cross with Deneb at its head, just as in the book. He grinned in the darkness, unknown to those around him. He spoke the word *Deneb* in his mind and felt himself to be Adam, naming the new world around him.

He took his flashlight from his pack and read on. He'd

bought the book in a store he'd passed in San Francisco, using the Visa card his parents had gotten him. He'd also bought six blades for his saw, more sandpaper, and a San Francisco map, and had used the card to get more cash. He'd planned on building the whirligig there, but after a day of freezing in the fog and a night in a cheap hotel, unable to sleep for all the shouting and footsteps, he'd climbed back onto the bus that morning, heading south to San Diego. This would put the whirligig closer to the corner of the country and would put him in a warmer climate. He'd brought nothing long-sleeved. He hadn't mentioned this oversight, or any others, when he'd called his parents from the bus station in Los Angeles—they were dubious enough about the trip as it was. Just as in the first call he'd made, they'd barraged him with questions, reminders, and cautions. He'd half listened, curiously fingering his blond hair. He'd forgotten to bring shampoo and had washed it with soap, leaving it stiff as cardboard.

Setting out by eye from Deneb, he found Vega, then Altair. He hadn't realized before that individual stars had names. The book called these three "the summer triangle." He stared at Vega, the brightest, bluish white, and felt it stare back at him. They held the gaze like tango dancers, while the woman behind him snored obliviously. The trio of stars shone for him alone. By now he was accustomed to feeling separate from the other passengers. For them, the bus was an interlude; for him, it was home.

No other existence outside of travel awaited him. It was all as familiar to him as if he'd been riding for years: the scent of the bathroom, the menu at meal stops, the inevitable drinker far to the rear, the old woman in the first row who asked the driver to confirm that she was on the right bus every ten miles. It was an anonymous community, just right for him. But unlike the others, when he stepped off the bus, he'd remain in a world of nameless strangers. He looked out. Except that he now knew Deneb. And Vega. And Altair.

It was ten when the bus stopped in San Diego. Joints creaking, Brent clumped down the steps. The passengers gathered their luggage beside the bus, then scattered, their community disbanded. He alone remained outside, leaning his pack against a wall and fishing through his pockets for the paper. A young woman from Holland who'd gotten off in Santa Barbara had told him about youth hostels and had let him copy an address from her book. After the night in the San Francisco flophouse he was ready for a change, though not ready to use his Visa to stay somewhere like the Sheraton, as his parents had begged him. The trip was his to take, not theirs. The hostel—cheap, friendly, filled with students—sounded more interesting.

"Excuse, please."

Brent looked up. A short, mustached man with a suitcase stood before him. In one hand he held a tiny address book.

"I wonder, sir, if you can tell me where is this address in San Diego. My brother's house."

Brent knew he would be of no help. But when the man held the address book toward him, pointing to the bottom line with a pen, he instinctively stepped forward, bent over the book, studied the microscopic writing—then caught a flash of movement and turned. Behind him, a scruffy teenager had a hand on his backpack. Brent stared at him, speechless. He saw the door he'd come through. Then he glanced back at the first man, realized they were a team, saw no one to appeal to except two drivers at the far end of the station, and yelled "Leave me alone!" loudly enough that both drivers turned. The thieves exchanged a long look. The hand reluctantly released his pack. Then the pair skulked wordlessly into the night.

It took three packages of potato chips before Brent's heart slowed to normal speed. He was inside the station, squeezed onto a bench, surrounded by fellow travelers and safe. It dawned on him why animals lived in herds. He scouted the room's perimeter for predators, decided against walking to the hostel, marched outside, and got a cab. Through its window he saw the summer triangle following him and felt watched over.

The cab parked. Brent hefted his pack from the trunk and stood on the sidewalk after the cab left. The night air was warm. A bird was singing somewhere. Beside him, he now saw, stood a palm tree. He sighted up its long trunk, touched it, and felt he'd entered a different country. The impression was deepened when he walked up the steps and past the porch, where two women were sitting in wicker rockers and conversing in a language he couldn't place. Brent passed them and presented himself at the desk.

"Passport or visa, please," said the clerk. He was young, with a pungent English accent and a head heaped with black curls.

"Passport?" Brent was stunned. "I'm American."

"We only take foreign travelers," said the clerk. "The theory being, as I understand it, that this being your own country, you've already got yourself a place to stay."

Brent sighed conspicuously, wondered what to do, glanced at a couple huddled over a map, and saw that the hostel was simply a large house and that he was standing in a corner of its living room.

"Of course, it being as late as it is, and unlikely that anyone else will show up, and we being unusually empty as it happens, you might just convince me you're Canadian."

A smile flickered on the clerk's lips. Brent stared at him and slowly comprehended.

"What city was it you're from?" the man asked.

Brent racked his brain, then thought of the cyclist he'd met at the campground in Washington. "Prince George," he answered.

"And what's Canada's capital?"

Brent rummaged madly through his mind, in vain.

"Ottawa, right you are," supplied the clerk. "And what year did England wrest control of your fair country from France?"

Brent knew this fact was nowhere in his memory.

"Seventeen sixty-three, right again," said the clerk. He handed Brent a pen and gestured grandly toward the register. "Welcome."

He gave Brent a tour and showed him to the room he'd share with three other males. Floating up the stairway came the faint peeping of a concertina. Brent had glimpsed the player in the dining room, a bearded man, eyes closed, his fingers punching out the melody on their own. After coming out of the bathroom, Brent stood listening to the cheery, reedy sound. He envied the man his power to entertain himself and others. There seemed no end to his stock of tunes. He thought back to the cyclist, admirably self-contained as well, not simply with his dome tent and gas lamp, but with his Go game and his thick book on the subject. By comparison, his own life seemed unfurnished with skills and interests. He desired to become the man he was impersonating.

He woke to find himself alone in the room. He smelled bacon. Like gravity, the scent pulled him irresistibly downstairs. The hostel served a free continental breakfast. Those who'd bought their own groceries were cooking more substantial fare in the kitchen. Cautiously, he entered the fray, nonchalantly poured some coffee—a drink he'd tried only once—grabbed a pastry, and took a seat. A minute later a young man sat across from him and asked, "Where are you from?"

"Canada." Brent kept his voice low. He sipped his coffee, fought back a grimace, and reached for the sugar bowl.

"What part?"

"British Columbia," he mumbled, praying there were no Canadians present. He ate his sweet roll nervously. The lies were piling up: that he was a coffee drinker, a Canadian, and, most serious, that he was a mere tourist, not a convicted killer on a mission of repentance. Not only his every word, but his every bite and breath was counterfeit. Prison, where no pretense was needed, suddenly seemed the better choice.

His tablemate was German, a year older, traveling before starting college in the fall. Brent was amazed that he had no accent. After one year of French and three of Spanish, he could neither understand nor speak a sentence in either language. His companion mentioned that he'd just finished *Two Years Before the Mast* and would pass it on to him. Brent sensed from the boy's comments that he knew more about American history than Brent himself did. The boy was tall, with strawberry-blond hair. The two could be mistaken for each other at a distance. Brent studied him in secret admiration, thinking that he might easily have been born into his body instead, might speak his three languages and know all that he knew. When the German asked if he wanted to see the sights downtown with him, Brent at once abandoned his plan to start the next whirligig. A half-hour later they were boarding a city bus.

The Pacific in the distance, the red tile roofs, the palm trees and countless Mexican restaurants all made Brent feel gloriously distant from Chicago. Mexico was only twenty miles away according to the German boy. He introduced himself as Emil. They got off the bus at Balboa Park, headed for the San Diego Zoo, and spent the rest of the morning strolling through mesas, rain forests, and aviaries. Emil would be studying biology at his university and provided a constant commentary on bird plumages and migration, European snakes, the evolution of the elephant. Fantasizing he was beholding his own double, Brent watched raptly when Emil made sketches and jotted notes.

"I'm sorry if I'm talking too much," he said to Brent. "Both my parents are teachers."

"No problem."

"They would like me to become one as well. 'A teacher lives forever through his students.' These are my father's favorite words."

Brent suddenly thought back to Miss Gill, the mediator in Chicago, and her saying that the effects of an act traveled far beyond one's knowledge. He knew she'd meant harmful acts, like his. He saw now that the same could be said of good deeds, such as a teacher's years of inspiring. Everything we did—good, bad, and indifferent—sent a wave rolling out of sight. He wondered what his own accounting, generations later, would look like.

They ate lunch, watched a marimba duo and a sword swallower in Balboa Park, sampled the museums of photography and model railroading, then spent two hours in the natural history museum. Brent had never known anyone his age who went to museums voluntarily. He was strictly Emil's sidekick. Afterward, however, while exploring downtown, he asserted himself and abruptly entered a music store they were passing. He could still hear the concertina's merry burbling in his head. Ten minutes later he walked out with a harmonica and an instruction book. He'd try his hand at making his own music.

Dinner at the hostel was a boisterous affair, conducted in several languages. He and Emil had bought some frozen enchiladas, which they heated in the kitchen's overburdened microwave. It seemed strange to Brent to see men carefully mincing garlic and sautéing vegetables. He was a stranger to the stove. Nor did the dinner conversation at this table resemble anything heard in his house. Mixed in with descriptions of Sea World and the beach were long discussions of world affairs, sometimes in raised voices. Brent was surprised at how much the other guests both knew and cared. Politics had never come up at home. Brent listened unobtrusively as diners and topics came and went. Finally, he slipped out himself.

The concertina player was nowhere about. The house

seemed much emptier without him. Brent observed travelers writing postcards, recalled that he'd bought some, and realized he had no one he wanted to send them to. He was a planet on which there was no other life as yet. Then he felt the harmonica in his pocket and thought to himself, Let there be music.

He chose the back lawn, more private than the rockers on the front porch. He read the booklet's introduction ("The instrument you hold is a full orchestra in miniature . . ."), stared at the photo marked Figure 1-A, snorted at the player's jacket and cuff links, read three times the detailed instructions ("Raise your harmonica. Now moisten your lips. Fill your lungs, then partially exhale . . ."), set the instrument to his mouth, and produced his first note ("Congratulations . . ."). By the fading light, then by flashlight, he pored over Lesson One, trying to find C at the fourth hole without looking, tripping over the C scale's quirky pattern, laboring with scant success to get a single note instead of two. He put it away, discouraged, glaring at the words *Play Instantly!* on the booklet. He turned off the flashlight. He tilted his head, found the summer triangle, a familiar face to him now, and felt better.

In the morning he found a paperback copy of *Two Years Before the Mast* by his bed, with Emil's address written on the bookmark. He'd left very early according to the clerk. Brent looked as though he were leaving as well, tramping out the front door with his pack on his back after breakfast. Feeling a fraud, he walked three blocks, turned to the right, walked four more, and came to a park he'd glimpsed the day before. Here he could work on his whirligig undetected by the other guests.

He claimed a picnic table, laid out his tools like a surgeon, and flipped through his book. He made up his mind to vault ahead from the simplest style he'd built in Washington and decided on the spouting whale, operated by a propeller and rods. The book's previous owner had been there before him, leaving penciled annotations like footprints. The sight of them cheered Brent. He sketched the whale on wood, erased, revised, then realized Lea wasn't in it. He considered giving the whale her face, then painting her in its belly as Jonah, then looked through the book, saw a design with a mermaid, and decided to change its hair to black and transpose it to the top of the spout. He didn't know what had given him the nerve to try such an ambitious project. The sunny morning made anything seem possible.

By dinnertime, not even close to half-finished, he felt like a gasping marathon runner, wondering why he'd made himself do it. The whirligig ended up taking three days spent in trying to balance propeller blades, bending rods, threading rods, wasting wood, starting over, walking a mile and a half to a hardware store for supplies and advice. He learned the hard way to paint in the morning, so that the surfaces would be dry by the time he packed up at the end of the day. He swore at the book, then at himself for making foolish mistakes. It was the harmonica that saved him. Playing it during breaks and at night, improving at blowing through a single hole, progressing from "Hot Cross Buns" to "Tom Dooley" to "Twinkle Twinkle Little Star," he added drop by drop to his store of perseverance, which supplied both tasks.

Despite the difficulties, the whirligig was absorbing, blocking everything else from view. The characters from his first life—allies, enemies, potential girlfriends—who'd once loomed like giants were now barely visible, distant figures disappearing over the horizon. He still noticed the cars he'd lusted after and heard snatches of songs linked to that era. His reactions felt distanced and ghostly. He had no desire to revive that life. It had all been crumpled in the crash. He no longer gave any thought to his clothes. He was an outcast, part of no group, and no longer had anyone to impress. Only when the wind blew did he feel watched—by Lea, looking down on his work.

It was late afternoon when he finished it. After testing it dozens of times, he looked down at the book's instructions, took his pencil, and wrote in the margin, "Added mermaid from page 87 on spout," followed by the date and his name. He felt he was conversing with the book's former owner. He now faced the problem of where to set it up. He didn't think it would last long in a public park in a big city. Then he remembered seeing a set of wind chimes on the hostel's porch. He made his way back and asked the clerk if he could offer it as a gift, in thanks for being taken in.

"Sure. Bring a bit more life to the front." He viewed it. "But no need to go buying presents."

Brent mounted it then and there, trying out three different locations and making various minor adjustments. The wind that sprang up each afternoon was blowing, sending the whale's white spout up and down, with the mermaid on top like a bronc rider. No guests chanced to be out front. Brent snapped a photo and disappeared.

When the subject of its origin came up at dinner, Brent was as silent as the others. Afterward, though, on the porch, he was not. He claimed one of the rockers, took out his harmonica, and began work on memorizing "My Bonnie Lies Over the Ocean." It had been sung briskly back in grammar school, the refrain cheery and rousing. He now saw it for the lament that it was. Lea lay across an ocean no boat could cross. He practiced the song over and over, scratching into his brain the pattern of which holes to draw on and which to blow. He finally got it down, closed the book, faced Lea, and played it through perfectly. Champagne bottles are broken on ships' bows; this felt like the whirligig's christening. A couple sitting on the front lawn clapped.

Early the next morning Brent moved on.

Bellevue, Washington

It's the first day of fifth grade. Everyone wants to impress Miss Rappalini. Except me. I'm not really listening to her. Man, does that feel good.

She says something about starting our journals. I'm drawing the Seattle Mariners' logo on my desk. They're playing a game against the Yankees today. The pregame show starts in fifteen minutes. My radio is in my T-shirt pocket, hidden by my long-sleeve shirt. In thirteen minutes I'll begin working the earplug cord down my sleeve. When it comes out at the cuff, I'll tape it to my palm. Then I'll prop my elbow on my desk, lean my head against my hand, and stick the earplug in my ear. Paradise!

Suddenly, everyone's opening up journals. We're supposed to write about our summers. Great. My summer was like being sick to your stomach. First, you feel worse and worse. Then you think you might have to throw up. Then you *know* you have to. Then you do.

I write, "I had a wonderful summer." There's no way I'm going to tell her the truth. I try to think what else to say. I touch the radio in my pocket. I imagine that I'm the guest on Bob Baker's Mariners' pregame show.

ANNOUNCER: *Anthony, great to have you with us.*

ME: *Thanks, Bob. But call me Tony. My mother's the only one in the universe who calls me Anthony.*

ANNOUNCER: *Well, let's just hope she's not listening.*

ME: *Don't worry. She thinks sports fans are lunkheads and time-wasters. And she's specifically told me that your voice makes her fillings ache.*

ANNOUNCER: *Thanks for sharing that with us, Tony. Now then, tell us about your summer.*

ME: *Well, Bob, I had my birthday in June.*

Which is actually a lie. Nobody knows my real birthday. I was left at an orphanage in Korea. They must have just picked out a day. Not that I remember even being there. My parents adopted me when I was a baby. This birthday, I asked for a new baseball mitt, a remote-control car, a Nintendo, and a gift certificate to Sam's Sports Cards. I received two shirts, a microscope, a new music stand, and a Sarah Chang CD.

ANNOUNCER: *Sarah Chang, the young violin virtuoso, of Korean descent, like yourself?*

ME: *That's right, Bob.*

ANNOUNCER: *Rookie of the Year in ninety-two. An All Star every year since. Holder of single-season records in harmonics, triple stops, and left-hand pizzicato. The kind of kid who always goes out and gives a hundred and ten percent.*

ME: *That's her.*

ANNOUNCER: *And tell our listeners at home—do you play violin too?*

Do I ever. Suzuki lessons starting when I was four. Listening to the tapes day and night. A big party to celebrate when I finished Book One. Then came the violin camps in the summer, group recitals, more and more pieces to review, crossing the bridge to Seattle twice a week for lessons. And now Youth Orchestra's starting up again. It's not that I'm so good. I'm not. Some other kids my age who take lessons from my teacher are way ahead of me. But to my mother I'm not average. I'm Korean. I can do anything, *if I apply myself.* She can barely whistle, but who cares. She's pure American, from Kansas. Nobody expects her to know the Paganini *Caprices.* But me, I get up in the dark for my forty-five-minute practice before school, with my door open so she can hear. Then I do another forty-five minutes after school, while my friends are playing baseball in the street. I'd quit in a second, but she won't let me.

I write, "I played my violin a lot."

ANNOUNCER: *That's one tough training schedule.*
ME: *That's not all, Bob. My parents signed me up for science camp all July. Nine to three. It was practically as bad as school.*
ANNOUNCER: *And your father, isn't he a scientist?*
ME: *Right, Bob. An electrical engineer. And then there's my mother's grandfather, also named Anthony. He built the first radio transmitter in Kansas. They named me after him, to inspire me.*
ANNOUNCER: *Both wearing the same number, so to speak. Must make you proud.*

Actually, I'd rather be my sister, Kelsey. She's not named after anybody. She's adopted too, but from Peru. Talk about no pressure, except maybe to learn to spin llama wool. She's in the first grade and my parents still haven't made her pick an instrument yet. They say she's not mature enough. They also probably won't bug her about winning her class Scholarship Award the way they have with me.

I chew on my pencil for a while. Then I write, "I went to science camp and learned a lot."

ANNOUNCER: *What about on the leisure side, Tony?*

ME: *Well, Bob, I went to one Mariners game. One. They lost. And we took a family camping trip for the first time.*

ANNOUNCER: *Tell our listeners what it felt like. Were you nervous? Excited?*

ME: *Buying all the stuff at REI was fun. And learning how to set up the tent.*

Which I figured might come in handy if I ever wanted to run away from home. We only went a little north of Seattle. It was kind of like a practice trip. We were right on the water. It was great. Then I found two ticks on my throat. Then I couldn't sleep because my sleeping bag kept sliding off my mattress pad all night. But the worst part was the whirligig. It was a girl playing a harp, like in an orchestra. It was in this tree at our campsite. And since it was breezy weather that weekend, the girl's arms were almost always turning. So naturally my mother had to say, "Look how she practices all the time, Anthony. A musician has to be dedicated. That's how she'll get into Honors Orchestra. And then the Seattle Symphony." As if she's a real person. My mother took about twenty pictures of it, some with me underneath. I hated the guts of whoever put it there. When no one was looking I picked up a rock. I'm good at baseball, especially pitching. I threw it at the girl. I hit her. It spun the whole thing around, but it didn't break. My mother must have heard the sound. She caught me about to throw another rock. I was under arrest. I had to stay in the tent the whole rest of the day. Talk about breaking the pledge.

ANNOUNCER: *For our listeners who may not know, what is this "pledge" you're speaking of?*
ME: *Glad you asked, Bob. Basically, it's like the Pledge of Allegiance, except that it's only for people of Asian background. And you don't say it out loud, but only inside.*
ANNOUNCER: *Could you give us a taste of it?*
ME: *Sure thing, Bob. "I pledge allegiance to Sarah Chang and all other Asian-Americans that I will be quiet, hardworking, and polite, succeeding in all things through dedication—"*
ANNOUNCER: *So you, for instance, unlike the other kids, would never call Miss Rappalini "Miss Ravioli" behind her back.*
ME: *Exactly, Bob.*
ANNOUNCER: *Then throwing the rock, if I understand you, was breaking every commandment in the pledge.*
ME: *You said it, Bob.*

In my journal I write, "We went camping. It was fun."
After the trip, we had more and more arguments about practicing. My mother said I should play for longer since school was out and I had more time. Naturally, she had one of the whirligig photos blown up and framed. She took down a poster of Ken Griffey, Jr., with a bat on his shoulder to make room on my wall. Every day she'd say, "Remember the harp player, Anthony—always practic-

ing!" It was almost like I was John Henry, in that song with him racing against a machine.

ANNOUNCER: *There's a trivia question for our audience. Who won the track-laying race between John Henry and the machine?*
ME: *The machine. We sang it last year. John Henry dies.*
ANNOUNCER: *You, Tony, were in his spot. Tell us what happened.*
ME: *I didn't die, or I wouldn't be here, Bob. Instead, I dropped out of the race.*

My mother started working part-time. I was supposed to tape my practices when she was gone. She didn't always get around to listening to the tapes right away. Sometimes they'd pile up. I'd tell her I'd practiced, then give her a tape from a few days before. I was supposed to be working on this piece for a big recital in August. I just sort of quit. I tried not to think about it. I told my mother I'd be playing something I already knew at the recital. I'd gotten away with the tapes—so why stop? When I told her I was going to the park down the street, I was really out with Ronnie Sneed, sneaking under the country club fence, looking for golf balls. We'd clean them up and sell them to a junk shop. Then we'd use the money to play video games. Or buy candy. Or go to the movies. He's the one who taught me how to buy one ticket and see all the different movies at the multiplex. Including *Death of a Stripper*, rated R. Which is where one of the theater guys found us. Naturally, he called our parents. This was the day before the recital.

I get up and sharpen my pencil. Then I write, "I played the Bach Gavotte in D Major at a recital last week." Which is as much of a lie as the rest of the journal. My teacher, Mr. Mintz, was accompanying me on piano. I could tell he knew I wasn't ready by how slowly he started us off. Even so, right away, I forgot the two grace notes. Then I messed up on the trill and the G-sharp. Mr. Mintz started again, but I actually played worse the second time. My hands were sweating and the strings felt slippery. I forgot to play the repeat. Then I forgot the bowing. Then I forgot the notes. It was like a car breaking down. We quit without ever playing the second section. People made themselves clap. My mother just looked down at the floor.

ANNOUNCER: *Wow. A new American League record for errors committed in a single composition. Must have been tough facing the fans after that.*
ME: *Let's just say we didn't stay for the refreshments.*
ANNOUNCER: *Guess you have to just put it behind you and work twice as hard to get your skills up to major-league standards.*
ME: *Actually, Bob, that's not how it's worked out.*

I had a long talk with Mr. Mintz, alone. He's an old man. He didn't seem mad at me. I told him everything, even about the whirligig. Then he called my mother into the room. He told us this Chinese saying, about how rest gives strength to activity. That's why there's night after day. And winter after summer, when the plants stop growing. He said the whirligig worked the same way. If it turned all the time without stopping, it would break.

ANNOUNCER: *Do you remember Coach Mintz's exact words?*
ME: *You bet, Bob. "The harp player plays her harp. Then she rests. Then she plays again." He said he thought it was an excellent idea to have a picture of the whirligig on the wall, to remember this. Then he looked at my mother and he said, "After speaking with Tony, I believe that he's ready for a rest."*

I'd broken the pledge. Now my mother broke hers. After Mr. Mintz talked to her alone, she actually let me quit violin. She also promised she wouldn't talk about the sixth-grade Scholarship Award. It was wonderful. Almost too good to be true. But that's the thing about throwing up—it's yucky, but then you feel a lot better.

I stare at my journal. Then I write, "The summer turned out to be pretty good." I don't have to be the best anymore. I celebrate by erasing the *e* in *pretty* and putting in an *i*. We don't get graded for spelling in our journals. I look at the word and almost crack up.

Then I look at the clock. The pregame show is starting. I pretend to scratch under my shirt and start feeding the cord down my sleeve.

ANNOUNCER: *That's one heck of a plan, with the earplug and all. I'd say maybe you take after that famous great-grandfather of yours after all.*
ME: *Thanks, Bob. Maybe you're right.*

Apprentices

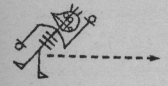

"He yanked her appendix out right quick. He said it was a time bomb, just fixing to explode. Then while he was poking around, he noticed something odd about her liver. . . ."

Brent was beyond commenting, nodding, or even looking in the woman's direction. She'd boarded in Phoenix. He'd said hello. In reply, she'd unrolled the immense panorama of her medical history, then had moved on to her husband—killed by doctors in 1981—then had switched to their Chihuahua, Pepe, whose string of sufferings exceeded Job's, and now had begun on the first of four daughters. Brent felt as if he'd turned on a TV to the Disease Channel. He aimed his gaze into the night. A full moon stage-lit the desert and revealed a troupe of saguaro cactuses. They were strangely human, their thick arms gesturing, each in the midst of a silent soliloquy. To Brent they looked ancient and wise. He'd have believed it if one had spoken. He studied them, wondering what they would say, and fell asleep with his head against the window.

The bus had a half-hour layover in El Paso. He went into the station to stretch his legs and was stopped by the sight of a missing-child flier. He peered at the picture of the dark-haired girl and thought of Lea, permanently missing. He felt like an escaped criminal who'd come face to face with his own "Wanted" poster. He was a fraud, posing as an innocent traveler, no better than the thieves at the San Diego depot.

He strode out the station door and was nearly turned back by the blinding light and blazing heat. He stopped, squinted, then stepped into a shaded doorway to adjust, like a diver decompressing. A time and temperature sign read 109°. He looked around. He'd never been in Texas. He liked not only being somewhere new, but knowing that no one else he knew had any idea where he was at that moment. He'd disappeared, shaken off all pursuers. A few doors down, a sidewalk preacher was declaiming. He was tall and red-faced, his shirt Arctic white and his forehead raining perspiration. Even his Bible seemed to be sweating. His back was to Brent, who couldn't make out his words. Then he turned.

" '. . . A fugitive and a vagabond shalt thou be in the earth,' " he shouted out.

He felt the man's tweezerlike eyes close upon him.

"That's what the Lord God said to Cain!" He wiped his face with a handkerchief and turned. Brent quickly retreated into the station, the man's words burning in his brain. Being a stranger in a strange land had suddenly lost its appeal.

The Corn Belt and Wheat Belt didn't do the country justice. Brent passed through a dozen unmentioned zones marked by various firsts: first business using Geronimo's name, first cowboy boots on a passenger, first appearance of catfish on a menu, first time being called "Sugar" by a waitress . . .

In East Texas the landscape's green deepened and the air hung heavy with moisture. He changed buses in Houston, opened Emil's cast-off copy of *Two Years Before the Mast*, and read all the way across Louisiana. He might almost have been reading his own life. Though the circumstances were different and the year was 1834, Richard Henry Dana had preceded him, setting out on a second existence of his own, leaving the lecture halls of Harvard for a life of travel as a working sailor. No more, Brent promised, would he complain about the bus after reading of the retching, fatigue, perennially wet clothes, and mortal dangers that the author endured. He forced himself to close the book, vowing to make it last.

88

The billboards announcing the Key Lime Pie Belt first appeared in Alabama, then proliferated across the Florida line. Brent got off in Tampa to transfer at 2:00 A.M., stiff-jointed and thirsty. He'd been riding for two days and nights. Though his ticket would take him all the way to Miami, the catalog of killings there recounted by the pair behind him had dimmed his desire for another big city. It was hot and muggy. He longed to go swimming. He consulted his map and decided to jump ship on Florida's Gulf coast. He boarded the next local bus heading south and was the only passenger to get off in the small town of Beale Beach. The sky was still black. He smelled the water. Staggering down the deserted main street, he turned down a side road toward a beach-front motel and was informed by the drawling clerk that check-in began at 3:00 P.M. Brent sleepwalked out. He trudged up the beach, shucked his pack, and fell asleep on the sand.

A mosquito in his ear was his alarm clock. He jerked awake, glanced around, and was startled to find two people strolling past him and the tide risen just short of his sneakers. It was nearly noon. His face felt sunburned. He roused himself, moved back from the water, then viewed the minuscule waves in dismay. When he'd lived in Atlanta they'd come to Florida, to Palm Beach, on the Atlantic side, where the waves had been monstrous and the water bracing. He waded in now and wondered if the water was actually hotter than 98.6°. He felt slightly foolish standing in it, the waves rubbing against his ankles like a cat. He'd had no idea that Florida's two coasts were so different. He considered catching the next bus out. Then he recalled a French woman in the San Diego hostel saying that the disappointments on her trip sometimes turned into her best experiences. Someone else at the dining room table had agreed. Brent didn't really feel like getting back on the bus. He slapped a mosquito dead on his arm and hoped the woman was right.

He ate a long lunch in the Sand Dollar Cafe, treated himself to both pecan and Key lime pie, and felt better. He explored the town, walked out on the pier, noticed that he was in the Ma'am and Sir Belt, and was surprised to find himself using these when he presented himself at a motel. The woman at the desk eyed his pack with suspicion. He sensed her scanning a list of possibilities and checking off "drug smuggler," "eco-terrorist," and "atheist backpacker." She asked to see his driver's license. He had none, hoped she wouldn't ask why, and produced the identity card he'd gotten in Chicago to take its place. He shamelessly loaded on the *Ma'ams*, then amazed himself by asking if there would be a Bible in his room. This gained him admittance to air-conditioning, a shower, a television, a telephone for ordering pizza, and a sagging bed.

He woke to the sound of his neighbor's TV, which had

blared ever since Brent had arrived. He turned on the radio to drown out the noise. The station it was set to was playing Dixieland. Brent had rarely bothered with jazz. It was unintelligible, a foreign language. He lay back and listened, tried to follow the trumpet's line, then the clarinet's, then began flipping through the whirligig book, came to the drawing of the marching band—and knew he'd found his next project.

He reached over to the night table for a bookmark. The piece of paper in his hand turned out to be a note from the maid. It read, "I hope your stay is a pleasant one. Trisha."

She'd put a circle, not a dot, over the *i* in her name, suggesting someone young. He pondered the message, knew that it was really a disguised request for a tip, but felt like taking it at face value as a welcome from a new acquaintance. His second life was short on friendship. He contemplated possible replies:

"I really like what you've done with the room."

"What's it like to clean motel rooms all day?"

"I'm a seventeen-year-old SWM, handsome, independent . . ."

"I accidentally killed a girl. I just had to tell someone."

In the end, he took the pad by the phone and wrote, "Dear Trisha: I appreciate your note. I'm completely alone." He stared at the words. He hoped she wouldn't take it as a come-on. He hadn't thought about girls for a long time and had no desire to meet her. He liked the idea of a disembodied conversation. He felt he could tell her more that way. He anchored the notes with a pen before leaving.

At the Sand Dollar he ordered a shrimp omelet, tried Tabasco sauce for the first time, overdid it, drank all of his water, then set off up the beach with his pack. Though his room was air-conditioned, he'd decided not to work there. He didn't want to face Trisha, didn't want anyone to see his tools, and didn't care to stay cooped up for three days listening to the laughter from his neighbor's sitcoms. The day was overcast and cooler. He marched on, hoping to escape all observers lest word of his strange activity get back to the desk clerk. The palm trees on his right, he noticed, looked different from those in San Diego. The black-headed gulls crying overhead were new to him also. The beach was all but empty. Summer, he realized, was the off-season here.

He left the town proper and eventually came to a boarded-up ice cream shop set next to a glass-strewn parking lot. "Open" was painted in large letters on one wall, contradicting all evidence to the contrary. There was a chain across the cracked drive that led to the beach-front road. Beside the building were three initial-scarred picnic tables, once shielded from the sun by a metal frame-work that had lost nearly all of its fiberglass panels. He'd needed a table of some kind to work on. Now he needed shade. He looked around, then collected palm fronds, stood on one of the tables, and stretched to lay them across the metal bars, feeling as resourceful as Robinson Crusoe.

He drank one of the three cold sodas he'd brought and set to work. He heard an occasional car on the beach-front road, hidden by trees and a bluff. No one passed before him on the beach. It was almost too private a site, and slightly eerie. Looking up at the menu still posted on the wall, he felt like a misplaced customer, a Rip Van Winkle who'd awakened to find himself in a deserted world. When the wind kicked up and blew off half his fronds, the sky darkened, and a sudden deluge soaked him, he wondered if he was the storm's only witness. He dragged his pack under the table, then sat down beside it.

The rain passed as quickly as it had come. He emerged feeling cooler, replaced the fronds, and returned to work. The whirligig featured a drummer, a trumpet player, a clarinetist, and a man with a trombone. It was a leap beyond the spouting whale, with more figures, a six-bladed propeller, and a much more complex system of rods and pivots that made the instruments dip and rise as if the musicians were marching. Brent wasn't put off by the lengthy instructions and actually looked forward to a long project. What would he do with himself otherwise? The numbered steps were his manual for living, always telling him what to do next, his only guideposts in the wilderness. For the first time, he'd read them through closely, beginning to end, before starting in. This time, too, he managed to sidestep several of his earlier mistakes and no longer felt his tools contained mischievous spirits bent on thwarting him. He'd bought a new file in San Diego, a four-in-hand, with four different surfaces. He enjoyed its heft and admired its design. It came as a surprise to find himself harboring such feelings toward a tool.

He decided to make Lea the clarinetist, painstakingly sawed out the figure, then ate the sub he'd brought. He took a break and flopped in the water. Then he read from his star book's first chapter, studying the four drawings of the earth in its circuit around the sun. The tilt of its axis caused the Arctic to receive sun all day and night in the summer illustration, while Antarctica stood in darkness. He reread the captions, then the text below, and for the first time comprehended why there were seasons. Winter and summer, the solstices and equinoxes, the change in where the sun rose and set all derived from the earth's angled axis—and all suddenly made perfect sense. He pored over the illustrations, confirming and glorying in his understanding. Why hadn't he learned this sort of useful information in school? He read on. He'd been reborn after the crash. He would give himself a new education, starting at the beginning.

He added more fronds to block the sun as it moved west, until there was no room to add more. The sun's glare and his hunger finally drove him back. He packed up his things and walked through the water, halted by a score of strange shells on the way. The sight of fellow humans ahead was pleasing. He looked forward not only to the food but to the friendliness of the Sand Dollar. He stopped in his room first and took a shower so cold it seemed to turn his skin inside out. Then suddenly he remembered the notes. He shut off the water, walked out dripping, and snatched up the sole piece of paper on the table. The handwriting was slanted and unfamiliar.

"Trisha don't work today. No one's alone with Jesus."

He felt slapped rather than comforted by the second sentence. He vowed not to reveal himself again, tossed the note into the trash, and got dressed, thinking back to church. Religion, as practiced by his parents, was a social rather than a spiritual affair, the choice of which Methodist church to attend very similar to the choice of what car to buy and be seen in. Neither the sermons nor the Bible had seemed to intersect with his own life. He had no singing voice, had lip-synched the hymns, and, despite the note's claim, had felt conspicuously alone in church. He headed outside.

The Sand Dollar's tippy, varnished wood tables were nearly all free. He took a seat over in the corner, his usual spot.

"How's my little baby today?"

The words were called out by the grandmotherly waitress who'd served him at lunch the day before.

"Pretty good," he replied, though no answer was required.

She fluttered over, a plump angel bearing water. "There you go, honey. You already know your order?"

To speak and be spoken to nourished him. He knew she called everyone "baby" and "honey" but enjoyed the illusion of his specialness. Her worried comments on his skinny looks inspired him to order the complete roast beef dinner. Other diners began to drift in. He recognized a few. He felt almost like a regular, outranking a couple who entered and asked for a menu, unaware it was painted on the wall. While waiting, he wrote a postcard to Emil, even though he wouldn't be back in Germany to read it for another month. His food arrived. He read his star book while eating, glanced at the setting sun, then had an inspiration. He slid his chair back into the corner, sat up straight, felt his head bump the wall, and made a tiny mark with his pen on the sill where the sun first touched the horizon. Tomorrow he'd make sure to be there at sunset.

It was already stifling by the time he returned to his workplace the next morning. His fronds blocked the sun, his repellent turned back the mosquitoes, but there was no escape from humidity. Any exertion slicked his body with sweat. Luckily, he wasn't swinging a sledgehammer but applying a speck of white paint to an eye, sanding a sharp corner, tapping in a brad. The musicians were only ten inches high. He lost himself in their miniature details and found the work meditative. There was no reason to rush.

A breeze blew in off the water after lunch. At the same time, in the opposite direction, a gaggle of children flew out of the palms up the beach and splashed into the water. Brent's head jerked up. There were seven or eight of them, all black, all grammar-school-aged except for one older girl. They played in the water, threw sand, waded out. Then one of them spied him, called to the others, and led a noisy charge to investigate. Brent's sanctuary suddenly squirmed with life.

"He got shade in here!"

"What you making?"

"Can I paint?"

"You need me to help?"

He began to explain what a whirligig was, then heard his harmonica being blown. While negotiating its safe release, he caught the rasping sound of his saw. He felt like a substitute kindergarten teacher. He finally took the harmonica and blew full-force to get everyone's attention. Then he held up the illustration of the marching band whirligig in the book and let one of them blow on the finished propeller, sending it circling smoothly.

"Cool!"

"My uncle plays the harmonica."

"I know how to saw."

"Make me one!"

He wished he had some extra wood for them to play with, but he'd barely enough to finish this project. He had plenty of nails, though, and let one boy hammer some into a chunk of driftwood. At once there was a tussle over the hammer. He ended up forming a line and issuing five nails to everyone in it. He tried to remember where he was in his work.

"Where you from?" the older girl asked.

"Chicago," Brent answered. He took up his pliers.

"Why you making that thing, anyway?"

He twisted a loop in the end of a rod. The outlandishness and mystery of his undertaking suddenly struck him afresh. His eyes lost their focus on his work. "Just for fun." His voice held no conviction.

A boy peered at him point-blank. "Are you famous?"

Brent smiled. "Nope. Not at all." He looked around for his wire cutters. "You're about the only ones in the world who know I make these."

They drifted back to the water after a while, then vanished into the trees. Brent worked until late, turning his back to the sun when it sank below his palm fronds. Then he remembered that he had a date with it at the Sand Dollar. He arrived just in time, snagged his table, tuned out the young waitress's recitation of specials, and watched the sun touch the water just to the left of his mark on the sill. He beamed. It had moved to the south. This made sense—it was July, past the summer solstice.

"Do you need a few minutes?" the waitress repeated.

"Yeah."

He sensed she was baffled by his grinning.

Back at the motel, his neighbor's TV was on. Brent

pictured a skeleton still gripping the remote. Retreating to the beach, he pulled out his harmonica, played the six songs he'd memorized, then moved on to "I've Been Working on the Railroad." It grew dark. He lay back, watched the stars emerge, greeted by name the constellations he knew, then took out a scrap of red cellophane. He'd begged it from a florist near the bus station in Mobile and now fitted it over his flashlight with a rubber band. His star book had said this would ease his eyes' adjustment between light and darkness, handy when studying a star map at night. It seemed to help. He worked the southern sky, glancing between his book and the heavens, and added Scorpius to his list, with its poised, potent, sickle-shaped tail and the red star Antares at its heart. He finally closed his book and just gazed. He glimpsed a falling star in the west, like a match scratched against the sky, then returned to his room and rationed out three chapters of *Two Years Before the Mast* before going to sleep.

The children didn't appear the next day. The following day, four of them returned. He took a break, went swimming with them, and learned from a little boy that the ridged, orange shells were called lion's paws and that the birds diving into the water were terns. He didn't mind apprenticing himself to a third-grader. In gratitude, he let the boy drill holes in a long finger of plywood.

He finished the whirligig that afternoon. The only wind to test it with was provided by the lungs of his four

assistants. Cheeks ballooned out, they blew on the propeller. The red-jacketed band stirred to life. The first
musician raised his trumpet. The trombone dipped. The
drumstick rose. Lea lowered her clarinet. It had been
Brent's idea not to have their instruments rise and fall
in unison. The staggered motion gave it a more exciting
rhythm. He studied it, pleased. His breathless audience
agreed. He grabbed the camera from his pack and put
them in the picture.

He drilled two pairs of holes in the base and threaded
through two lengths of brass wire. Then he moved one
of the picnic tables, climbed up, and secured the whirligig
to the top of the metal framework, across a corner.

"You don't want it?"

"It's not for me," he said. He stepped down off the
table and admired it. "It's for you. Nobody else comes
here. You'll be the only ones who know it's there."

"What about when a hurricane come?"

Brent hadn't thought of this. "Do you get hurricanes?"

"Lots of 'em!"

"We don't neither."

"I ain't scared of 'em."

"It gonna tear that thing up!"

Brent scanned the Gulf. The sky held no clouds.
He thought back to the storm that had appeared out of
nowhere and drenched him a few days back. No doubt
another would blow in someday with winds strong enough
to wreck his handiwork. There was nothing he could do

about it. He was sure Lea's mother would understand. No matter what happened, she would have the photo of the four grinning faces around the marching band.

He began packing up. Then he noticed the boy who'd drilled holes through the strip of plywood. He'd put a nail through one of the holes, hammered it into the side of a table, and was now blowing on the wood. This improvised propeller budged, then stopped. He blew again, then pulled out the nail and hammered it through a different hole.

Brent watched the boy at work—and cast off all worry about hurricanes. After the storm, new whirligigs would appear.

San Diego, California

We were at opposite ends of the house and of the life span. A hall, a stairway, the den, the dining room, and another hall all lay between us. But even up in my room with the door shut, even listening to the radio loud or looking at my old dolls and scrapbooks, my mind a million miles away, I was conscious of my grandmother's presence. I was always waiting, listening, imagining. Always aware someone was dying downstairs.

When it was just the two of us home, the entire house seemed to resound with her heartbeat. I'd plug in the portable intercom by my bed and count the minutes until my mother came home from errands or my father from the university. Fortunately, my grandmother slept a lot. My mother assured me she was doing just that when she left to go shopping one day in July. I was reading a collection of Anne Frank's father's letters, then realized that I'd stopped and was just staring at the intercom. Five seconds later the sound of my grandmother clearing her throat came through the speaker, a long overture of scraping and swallowing. My heart began to race.

"Rachel . . ."

I closed my eyes. Rachel was her sister, long dead.

"No. Deborah."

Her daughter. My mother.

More throat-clearing. "Deborah. Please come."

The words catapulted me off the bed. Her moment had arrived. Impossible, I answered back. Everyone said the chemotherapy had helped. I flew down the wood stairway, pushed by duty, pulled back by dread. I loved my grandmother, but I did not love shots, bedpans, puking, or the sight of stitches. I was fifteen and still hated taking pills. I rushed down her hall and opened the door.

"What's the matter?" I almost yelled the words.

She was still in her pink nightgown, propped up in her old canopied bed. Her head turned slowly from the intercom to me. "Jenny. I called for Deborah."

"She's gone out." I scanned her. The skin hung in accordion folds on her cheeks and drooped below her eyelids but didn't seem to be flushed or pale. Her small eyes were bright.

"Why did you call? What's wrong?"

"What?"

She refused to admit that she needed a hearing aid. I sat on her bed and bellowed as if she were across the Grand Canyon. *"How do you feel?"*

"Weak," she said. "No strength."

Talk like this was a change for her. Until lately she'd always answered "Like Jesse Owens" or "Like Joe DiMaggio." She was an amazingly positive person for someone who'd been in Auschwitz. I took her hand and stealthily looked, for the thousandth time, at the place on her wrist where her number had been tattooed. She'd had it removed, and seemed to have done the same with her memory of that time. She never brought it up and wouldn't answer my questions.

"What do you need?"

"Is Joseph home?" she asked in return.

"He's still at work."

She looked down and mumbled her disappointment. Then her head rose. Her eyes scuttled over me. "Do you drive, *kindelah?*"

"Yes, Grandma."

"So grown-up you are, Jenny." She viewed me with pride. "So tall. Such beautiful brown hair." She smiled. "Let's go, then."

I stared back at her in panic. "But I don't have a real license yet. Are you kidding? Go where?"

"Somewhere."

I knew where, from my parents' experience. To a pharmacy way out on El Cajon where the trustworthy son of a friend of hers worked. Or on a scavenger hunt for a brand of cracker that hadn't been made in twenty years, or a cheese she remembered from back in Poland. Nothing had tasted good to her since the cancer treatments had started.

"Grandma, listen! I'll call my father. He'll stop by on his way home. What do you need?"

"This he can't bring me. First, help me dress."

"But I only have a learner's permit," I stammered. "An adult always has to be with me."

"I'm not an adult? I'm not old enough?" She gave a laugh, which started her coughing. Her left hand pointed at the closet while she hacked.

"The navy blue dress," she got out at last. Her accent was still thick. Then again, Yiddish was her first language, English her sixth. "And the black shoes, Jenny dear."

Practically all of her shoes were black. I stood before her clothes and bit off two fingernails. With my mother gone, that left only the old Toyota, a manual. I hated shifting. I turned around.

"But, Grandma, my mother can take you. She'll be back in two hours. At—"

"No more waiting," she declared. "Waiting is dangerous when you're my age."

I gathered her clothes and helped her get into them. The temperature was in the nineties, but she insisted on that wool dress, broiling and ancient. Likewise on a wig from the Eisenhower era to hide her chemo-caused baldness. Though our house was quite modern, with lots of glass and odd angles, my grandmother's clothes and furniture made her room into a time machine. From her heavy, claw-footed dresser I got the gold brooch that she asked for. Then I helped her up and put her cane in her hand. The bend of its handle matched her back. We inched our way down the hall.

"We go left here, Grandma. It's shorter."

I was now a full head taller than she was. I pulled her gently to the left and winced at the sight of her baggy dress. She'd lost weight and height in the past few years. I let her rest.

"No hurry," I said. It was a week since she'd been out of her room. Only a year before she'd lived in her own apartment, walked to the grocery, taken cabs to visit her friends. When my mother insisted she move in with us, her doctor visits increased but the rest of her world began shrinking—first to the house, then to her room, and finally to her bed. Leading her out the front door, I couldn't help but think how little she resembled the woman who'd walked in the summer before.

"Grandma, where are we going?" Judging by her clothes, it was someplace fancy.

"I'll show you."

The car was sitting out in the driveway and was hot as a sauna inside. I opened the doors to cool it off, got her seated, and turned the key. The engine gave a growl like a guard dog and died. It took two more tries to get it going. The air-conditioning didn't work, naturally. I let the engine warm up a long time while I looked down at the gearshift knob, its handy shifting pattern worn away. For a full minute I searched for reverse. When I found it, it turned out to be fourth. I stalled, which saved us from ramming the garage door. I hunted some more, reminded myself of my excellent record in driver's training, found reverse, and shot back out of the driveway at a speed that threw both of us forward. Thank God the car was too old to have airbags. I fiddled with the gearshift, found first, and proceeded down the street as nonchalantly as possible. I realized my grandmother was eyeing me.

"Maybe it's better I wait for—"

"Grandma, *I can drive*. Just tell me where you need to go."

She knew San Diego well, which was good since I was giving all my attention to finding the clutch with my floppy sandals and getting into first without stalling. We drove a long way down Morena. The breeze from the open windows kept me cool, until my grandmother had me roll hers up. We drove along Mission Bay, then reached Old Town.

"Stop!" she called out.

I slammed on the brakes. So did the ten cars behind me. There was honking. I was stopped in the middle of the street. I wanted to yell, "My grandmother *told* me to!" Cars zoomed around me. Mine had stalled and didn't want to start again. I could feel the blood rise into my cheeks. I glanced furiously over at my grandmother and found her staring at a white-barked tree.

"All right, Jenny dear. Go on."

I was speechless. She was completely unaware of what was happening. I felt like getting mad at her, but then I saw that her face had that unfocused look it had more and more lately. She was often confused or lost in her thoughts. How could I blow up at her for that?

I got the car going. I put it into first and took off, trying to forget the whole scene.

"Turn right when you come to the furniture store."

She navigated by landmarks, in Old World fashion, not by blocks and street names. I turned. My bangs were damp on my forehead. We entered downtown. Too many cars and buses. My hands were sweaty both from heat and nervousness.

"Next time you want me to stop, Grandma, give me a little warning," I said.

"What?"

I was repeating myself at a higher volume when she suddenly called out, "Here it is!"

I almost braked, then looked in the mirror. Nothing was behind me. I stopped.

"Go back a little."

I rolled my eyes, fumbled with the gearshift, found reverse, and backed up. We were somewhere on Fourth. She was staring at a little Chinese restaurant. Cars were coming. I put on my turn signal, then the warning lights just to be safe.

"Again it's changed," she said. The wave of traffic washed around us. She sat and stared.

"Grandma, there are restaurants closer to home. With good Jewish food—"

"Keep going, *kindelah*."

I don't think she heard me. She looked back at the restaurant as we left.

"Keep going where?"

"Straight. I'll tell you."

I thought of the time she'd led my mother starting and stopping all over town in search of a phantom bakery. Why had I agreed to this? We drove down to Broadway, then turned left. The neighborhood started making me nervous. I checked the gas, something I now remembered you were supposed to do before you left. I had a quarter tank. We turned up Thirtieth.

"Are you sure you know where we're going?" I asked.

"At the brick church there, make a right turn."

I turned. She stopped me a few doors down in front of a stucco house shedding paint. Two little black girls stared at us from behind a palm tree in the yard.

"Grandma, are you lost? There's no stores on this block."

She was silent. Then she said, "Rachel lived here."

I gazed at the house. My middle name is Rachel, given

in honor of my grandmother's sister. Strange, I thought, that my parents had then given me a first name like Jennifer, as far from the Old Testament and the Old Country as you could get. Then again, maybe that was the point. To put Poland and Hitler and the camps behind them. To blend in for a change, instead of sticking out. They'd done this so well—never going to synagogue, avoiding speaking of my grandmother's experience, even getting a Christmas tree—that they propelled me in the opposite direction. I'd enrolled myself in Hebrew school, older than all the other students, and had nervously, proudly chanted my portion of the Torah at my Bat Mitzvah in May. I'd read every grisly account of the Holocaust I could find and gave all my birthday money that year to Simon Wiesenthal's Nazi-hunting group. Never, I'd vowed, would I visit Germany. My mother warned me that I was too serious and didn't smile enough to attract boys.

"Grandma?"

"Go now, *kindelah*."

I got back on Thirtieth and headed north. We were nearing my grandmother's old neighborhood. At the red light at University she began pointing like a tour guide.

"That building there, that was a pharmacy. We used to have our ice cream there. You couldn't keep ice cream at home, not then. It would melt in the icebox. And there's the theater!"

The old Fox North Park was still standing, like a

Mayan pyramid overgrown by jungle. I caught "Tom Cruise" on the same marquee that had probably advertised Charlie Chaplin.

The light changed. I was not surprised to find my grandmother taking us on a detour to her old house, two blocks over, on Kansas. I found it and idled. It was hard to believe that the squat white bungalow before us, with its torn screen door and dead tree by the walk, was the site of my mother's golden childhood, my grandfather's neighborhood croquet tournaments, the boisterous family get-togethers I'd heard of. Two seagulls circled above it like vultures. The house looked abandoned. Maybe it was.

"Grandma, I'm going to run out of gas if we keep this up."

She mumbled something—not in response to me, I realized. I cocked my ear. She was speaking in Yiddish. I only know a few words and had no idea what she was saying. She went on and on, facing the house, one hand on the gold brooch she was wearing. My eyes skipped from the sagging awning to the littered porch to my grandmother's face. Her eyes were closed, her lips still moving. Then she was silent. Then she said, "Please go."

I put the car into first and moved on. Stopping at a light, I saw ahead a little deli that I knew she liked. It dawned on me that she'd been leading us there. I was suddenly feeling hungry myself. We approached. I slowed to grab a parking place.

"Why are you stopping?" she asked. "Back home now."

"But Grandma, you never—"

She didn't hear.

"Thank you, *kindelah*. Very much."

"But we never got what you wanted!" I shouted.

Her head wobbled toward me.

"Where did you want to go?"

She looked puzzled. "To my house, where we just come from. To Rachel's house, God give her rest. To the stationery store we had, twenty-six years, until Jacob died."

I pictured the Chinese restaurant. I swallowed.

Then I thought of our first stop. *"What about the tree?"*

"A birch tree," she said. "There were very many birches in Poland where I grew up. The white bark. So beautiful." She inhaled deeply and wiped her eyes. "All these I wanted to see. A last time."

I was the driver but hadn't understood the journey. All at once I could barely see for the tears. I gripped the wheel tightly with both hands, trying to keep control of both the car and myself.

"But you're getting better, Grandma! You've got lots of life left!" I was doing my best to convince both of us.

She shook her head.

"Some things, *kindelah*, you know inside."

The brooch, I now remembered, had been a gift from my grandfather, presented at their fortieth-anniversary party. Had the blue dress been a favorite of his too, back in the years when it fit her?

We drove without speaking. We passed close by the apartment house she'd lived in before joining us. She said she didn't need to see it. But one block later her hand came up.

"Turn at the mailbox there. One more stop."

We were in a residential neighborhood, older and well kept. Half a block down she asked me to halt, then to turn around to put the car on the other side of the street. We idled in front of a two-story house with a fanlight over the door and a porch occupied by four rockers.

"I stop here for me and for you," she said.

I couldn't see the link to either of us. *"Why here?"*

She pointed a shaky finger to the left.

"The toy?" I asked.

She nodded. Mounted on the corner of the low porch wall was a whirligig, its propeller turning in the late afternoon breeze. I studied it. It was a figure of a whale, with a white triangle that was supposed to be its spray. The spray moved up and down above the blowhole. On top of the spray sat a black-haired woman.

"Look," said my grandmother.

We stared at it. The breeze picked up, making the spout clack up and down like a sewing machine needle. I glanced at my grandmother. She was smiling.

"Somebody," she said, "I don't know who, said there shouldn't be laughing after Auschwitz. That nobody could ever want to laugh again after the things that happened there." She rotated her head toward me. "But I was there, *kindelah.* Yes, very terrible. What I saw you should never dream. But I can also tell you that all those that died want that we should have a life with laughing. Not sad all the time, always reading books about Nazis and men who like killing. They want us to laugh all the laughs that were taken away from them."

I looked at the whirligig. But I was sniffling, not laughing.

"People are not all Hitler, *kindelah.* People are very good also, like the one who made this wind toy to give happiness to everyone who pass. People are good—even some Germans. When the bad memories came back in my head, here I walked to remind myself of this. This, not the other, I want to remember when I think my thoughts before I die. This I tell you, who have the permit for learning. I'm old. I have the permit for teaching."

I leaned across and threw my arms around her. It was a long time before I let go. Then we both gazed at the whirligig. I wiped my eyes and watched the whale spout. I glimpsed a smile on my grandmother's mouth. I felt it leap, like a spark, to mine. I turned off the car's engine and rolled down all the windows. I have no idea how long we sat there.

"Everybody Swing!"

Though his last name was Bishop, Brent felt like a rook, riding north on I-95, making another end-to-end chess move along the country's perimeter. He traversed the Alligator, Plantation Tour, and Robert E. Lee belts, then tried to sleep through Washington, Baltimore, Wilmington, Philadelphia, and Newark, the steaming streets and long skeins of graffiti magnifying his yearning for Maine. He transferred in New York at the Port Authority—the one place his father had urged him to avoid—and managed to hold on to his wallet and his life. The bus rolled past the exit for Milford, Connecticut, where he'd lived for two years. He looked out but didn't recognize anything, then forgot to get off in New Haven and call his grandmother, as he'd promised he would. He changed buses again in Boston, where he had an aunt and uncle and cousins, none of whom he desired to see. They were his past. The bus crossed a bridge, high and arched like a silver rainbow. A sign welcomed him to Maine. Brent stared out. This was his present. He stepped off into it in Portland.

It was 5:00 P.M. He strolled Congress Street and found his way to a bed-and-breakfast, the first he'd ever stayed in. He was primed to like it, but found it too similar to a small dinner party with strangers, his overly sociable hostess interviewing him about his trip with great interest and trying to get him to converse with the other guests at breakfast. The simplest questions forced him into lies. He preferred the less demanding social life of the bus and restaurants and motels. He'd have rather been out in the country as well, waking to the ocean instead of to the garbage truck below his window. He decided to move on, got a ride with one of the guests who was heading north, glimpsed a billboard for a campground on Casco Bay, and climbed out in the village of Weeksboro.

A series of signs led him toward the camp, taking him past a small grocery, where he stopped to replenish his food supply. He came to the Town Hall, then the village green, and stopped before a poplar tree, its leaves shaking and shimmering in the breeze, the ancestors of all whirligigs. Nearby stood a statue of a Civil War soldier. Brent approached as if he'd been summoned and found himself reading through the list of Weeksboro's fallen Union soldiers. The past was palpable here, a feeling that deepened when he detoured through the cemetery and found a slate headstone dated 1798. People, he noticed, had died young in the past. He thought of Lea. Many graves belonged to children. Pushing on, he passed between two white churches glaring at each other across the street, then turned left onto Bolton Road, and half a mile down reached Howlett's Campground. It was privately owned, a fact made obvious by the continuing parade of hand-painted signs:

"Welcome! Glad You Found Us! —Cliff & Vera."

"Free Firewood, Showers, and Ping-Pong. Also Free Fog, Rain, and Mosquitoes."

"Park At Any Unoccupied Site, Then Check In At Office."

"Office Hours: From Whenever We Feel Like It Till Whenever We Don't."

He looked at the Prussian blue sea while he walked, half surprised it wasn't labeled with a sign. Striking out down a path to the water, he surveyed a sandy cove, then returned and passed through a grassy camping area with many free spots but no privacy. He continued on and found a site more to his liking among the trees, with a table, a barbecue, and seclusion. He could see none of the other campers. There would be no need to hide his work, a physical and psychological luxury.

He pried off his pack, dug out his tent, and strung his

rope between a tree and a table leg. The tube of orange plastic hung on this, becoming triangular when he climbed inside and unrolled his sleeping bag. He lay down, listening to the wind and the waves. Strange, he thought, that he'd kept to the coasts. Lea's mother hadn't required this. Was it because he'd come from Chicago, near the center of the country? He'd certainly fled as far as he could, turning his gaze away, out to sea. Each of his four vantages had been different. He inhaled the air, delightfully cool and sharp-tipped with evergreen scent. "I'm in Maine," he said aloud, then confirmed this astounding fact by naming in order every city he could remember on the four bus trips that had brought him there, his geographical Genesis.

He walked to the office to check in. It was empty. The date, tide times, and weather report had been written on a chalkboard. Past issues of the Portland *Press Herald* lay on a table next to a sign reading: "Please Place Most Recent On Top." Brent began to wonder if the Howletts' small universe was entirely self-service. He opened a paper to the weather page, studied the national map, then checked the details for Seattle, San Diego, and Tampa. He pictured his whirligigs in their respective weathers. He almost felt he could look out through them and see people passing and birds overhead. He moved on to other distant scenes—postcards sent by previous campers. They were tacked to a corkboard, overlapping like shingles, many with their messages facing out. He read them all, sampling other lives, hoping for a hint on where to point his own. Nearby was a shelf marked "Book Exchange," another *camera obscura* offering views of the campers' lives: *Getting Organized, All for Love, The Best of Charlie Brown, Codename: Attila.* He was leafing through the latter when a white-bearded man in overalls strode in.

"Put one in, you can take one out. Anything else I can do for you?"

Brent savored his strong Maine accent. "I just came to check in. I'm in number 18."

"Back among the spruces."

Brent had thought they were pines. He made a note of this.

"That's a real good site for building your wrist muscles."

Brent was baffled.

"From slapping mosquitoes." The man opened his registration book. "That table there in 18 is new. The old one had more names on it than the Constitution. Went to the dump and found half a dozen perfectly good two-by-eights. Just needed a few rusty nails pulled out. The Lord doth provide. And the dump's where He does it. Most folks don't realize that."

Brent signed in. The man glanced around.

"I built half my house and all of this office from what I picked up there. Right down to the doorknobs."

Brent looked but could find no sign of the room's Frankenstein-like origins.

"Helps keep the price down. Ten dollars a day. How long would you be staying with us?"

"Three or four days."

"All summer, you mean."

Brent stared. The man gave no sign of jesting.

"No, just a couple of days."

"In Maine, lad, a couple of days in July *is* summer, beginning to end."

Brent ambled back to his camp, noticed the table's fresh coat of red paint, and vowed to be careful with his drill and saw. He felt anxious to start. He made a sandwich, decided to pick his next project while he ate, then couldn't find the whirligig book. Three times he checked all his pack's compartments. He'd been reading it coming into Portland. He realized he must have left it on the bus. He pictured it traveling on without him, crossing into Canada perhaps, inspiring someone to build a string of whirligigs that Brent would never know of.

He ate. Without the book he felt abandoned. Searching for it, he'd found he was very low on hardware as well as wood. A blue jay perched nearby, raucously panhandling him. He threw it some bread, thinking of fairy tales in which generous deeds are rewarded tenfold. No mountain of building supplies appeared. But in his mind there materialized the notion of a whirligig all his own, its plan found in no book in the world, its ingredients his remaining scraps and whatever he could scavenge, as the campground owner had. Surely there would be wood on the beach. He emptied his pack so as to use it as a carrier and marched toward the water.

The tide was out, its wares spread on wet sand. He picked up shells, fishing line, a length of rope, but little usable wood. The air was brisk. Two kayakers passed. He followed them enviously with his eyes and scouted the islands on the horizon. Coming to the end of the cove, he clambered up onto great slabs of granite and crossed them until he reached another beach. Here he gleefully picked through a long bargain bin of driftwood. He salvaged what he could from an old lobster trap, then discovered a pair of sand dollars, and was so intent on looking down that he didn't notice the woman seated against a rock until he'd almost tripped over her.

"Sorry," he said. Then he saw she had a watercolor set and was painting a crab shell beside her. "That's great," he added.

"Thanks." She brushed aside a long strand of gray hair and smiled up at him. "I'm not so sure it has the proper *ness*. What do you think?"

"What's 'ness'?" he asked.

She cleaned her brush. "Well, in the case of a crab shell, it would be roughness to the touch, lightness, hollowness . . ."

Brent bent down and judged. "Definitely."

"You think so? I'm glad." She glanced at him. "Do you paint?"

"Not really. Just a little bit, sort of." He thought of

his recent efforts—oversized eyes, drips running down the wood—and watched in wonder as she somehow ferried the crab's qualities to paper.

"A sort-of artist? That's me, too."

She was small and tanned, dressed in jeans and a moth-gnawed blue sweater. Brent thought her thick gray hair beautiful and wondered why his mother dyed hers.

"When I was your age I honestly dreamed of painting world-famous masterpieces." She mixed a pale orange. "Now I just paint." She did so in silence, then turned toward Brent. "This morning they played some Corelli on the radio. Composed in 1681. Don't you find it amazing that we're still listening to it, whole centuries later?"

Brent wondered how long his whirligigs would last. "I guess so."

"Amazing, and rare. The darkness swallows up most of us." She swirled her brush in a jar of water. "Not that he could know we still play it." She gestured toward a house, tall and white as a lighthouse, out on a point. "I very nearly walked outside and called, 'Hello, Arcangelo Corelli!' as loud as I could across the water. Is that crazy? Have you ever wanted to do that?"

He liked the way she spoke to him as to an adult. "I wouldn't call it crazy." He noticed that tied to her belt loops were short strips of bright fabric.

"What are those for?"

"Just for color," she said. "Why not? It's so dreary so

much of the year here." She looked up. "What sort of art do you do?"

"I make whirligigs." The words had come out without his permission. He wanted them back, then decided they were safe with her.

"Really. How unusual. And how wonderful." She studied him, grinning, her green eyes bright. "Perhaps you'll become their Arcangelo Corelli."

He smiled in return and sat on the sand. They talked for an hour, watching the gulls drop shells onto the rocks to crack them, then went their separate ways. By the time Brent returned, his pack was as full as Santa Claus's sack.

He laid his finds on the table and circled it. Ideas for whirligigs streamed through his mind like clouds, in constant metamorphosis. He scrutinized, weighed, and considered his ingredients while the sun dipped behind the trees. The mosquitoes emerged. He kept them at bay with a fire, then boiled water in his pot and dumped in half a bag of noodles. He poured off the water once they were done, sliced slivers of cheese on top with his knife, and felt himself a true French chef.

When the sky overhead became black, he left the woods in search of the stars. The main camping area flickered with fires. Two children were playing badminton by lantern light. Brent walked to the cove. He turned his head up and smiled, as if stepping into a party. The faces there were familiar. He'd missed them. The past several nights had been cloudy. He noticed at once how much higher the Big and Little Dippers were. Riding north from Florida, he'd covered twenty degrees of latitude. Part of the tail of Scorpius was now hidden below the southern horizon. He wondered what new stars he'd gained to the north. He slipped the red cellophane over his flashlight, opened his book to "Circumpolar Stars," and availed himself of his new view.

At dawn, a barking dog woke him up. He gazed toward the east out the tent's open end. Ten different reds quickly came and went, as if the sky were showing color samples. He studied the clouds' calligraphy, their foreign alphabet indecipherable. Then a dam of light burst and flooded the east, the sun rose, and the dawn display ended. It had all gone too quickly, like a dazzling amusement park flying past the bus window. "The darkness swallows up most of us." He heard the words spoken in the painter's voice, and suddenly saw his whirligig whole.

He started in then and there, and labored for three and a half days on it. He played his harmonica when he felt like a break and one day walked to the fabled town dump, returning with a small junk shop in his pack. The weather held clear. Each morning he woke to the purring of the lobster boats and each night went to sleep with *Two Years Before the Mast* and his flashlight. After lunch, he stopped in at the office and consulted the shelf of nature guides, searching for shells he'd found or birds he'd seen and writing their names in a notebook. In this way, he knew it was a black-capped chickadee that seemed to be chattering its congratulations at the moment he finished the whirligig.

He contemplated his work over lunch. It was three times the size of the others he'd built. The pinwheels on the front, snipped and fashioned from soda cans, stood becalmed. Likewise the dozen propellers made from golf-motif coasters, linoleum scraps, license plates, and lobster-trap slats. On the blades of one four-bladed model he'd painted Lea's four-part name. He considered the plywood rendition of her face. It was the most faithful of the four he'd made. For the first time, he'd given her a slight smile, painstakingly copied from her photograph. The head was large, giving him room to glue sea glass and red reflectors in her hair. Her skin glistened. Because it was Maine, he'd given the wood an extra coat of varnish. He'd drilled holes in shells and made her a necklace, hanging it over her head along with a set of wind chimes he'd rescued from the dump. Maine summers, like dawn colors, were brief. Darkness and winter predominated. Lea's life had been similarly short. But his clacking, flashing, jingling memorial would give off sound and color all year, holding back the tide of death. It was a kinetic gravestone, painted in ever-blooming greens and yellows and reds. Lea would not be swallowed up.

He walked to the cove. He wanted it mounted there and liked the idea that the first winds to come ashore from the Pacific, Gulf, and Atlantic would turn his whirligigs. He spent an hour hunting for a site that was far enough above high tide as well as safe from campers. There weren't any suitable trees available. He wondered if the campground owner would let him sink a pole in the ground. Then he looked across the water to the south and had a better idea—the painter's house, perched above the water on a treeless point, with no high tides or falling limbs or campers to worry about.

The whirligig was heavy, awkward to carry, and conspicuous in the extreme. He ignored the stares he drew in the campground, decided it would be easier to take the road, and was the cause of much braking and head-swiveling. The day was hot. His arm muscles burned. He shifted the contraption onto his head just as a breeze flowed over him, setting it ringing and spinning. It was engaged with the wind as if by a gear. Making his way up a hill, he listened to his respiration, his own wind surging in and out, and felt at one with the whirligig. The breeze picked up as he neared the woman's house, increasing the clatter and motion overhead. He spotted her weeding and supposed he must look like a demented relative of the Wright brothers. Nervously, he awaited her head's turning.

"Oh, my!" was all she could say at first. She got to her feet, jeans damp at the knees. Her agile eyes took in his strange cargo. Brent feasted on her smile of delight.

"It's wonderful! Truly." She stroked the chimes. "It makes me feel like a little child. And what painter in the Louvre wouldn't envy *that* power."

Brent rested it on a metal chair and watched her roam it with her eyes. A gust set it and the strips of bright fabric on her belt loops fluttering. He realized that they hadn't exchanged names. He liked the way she put important things first and left trivialities for last. He was glad he'd come.

"It reminds me of those Tibetan flags that flap in the wind, sending out prayers." She flicked a propeller and admired the sea glass. "It's a one-man band for the eyes. Bravo!"

"Thanks." Brent cleared his throat. "Actually, I was wondering if I could put it up here. If you wouldn't mind."

"You don't want to keep it?"

"I can't. And I made it to be here in Maine. By the coast." He stopped before he said more than he wanted to.

"I'd be thrilled. And honored." Her eyes sparkled. "Where do you think it ought to go?"

They strolled her grounds and toured her garden, discussing sites and a dozen other topics. An hour later Brent had removed a decrepit birdhouse from a metal pole and mounted the whirligig in its place.

"I promise you, no birds used that house," said the woman. "And when it goes to the dump, it might be just what some sculptor needs." They were drinking lemonade on the porch, both of them facing the whirligig and the long view up the coast. Cicadas droned in the sultry air.

"Now tell me—or don't, you've a perfect right not to. Is the woman someone real? I noticed the name."

Brent sipped. "She was." He sipped again, then held the icy glass to his cheek, partially hiding his face.

"She died in a car accident. In Chicago. In May."

The painter put her hand to her sternum. "Oh, no."

He was relieved they weren't facing each other. "It was my fault. I'm the one who killed her." He listened to himself as if to a stranger. "I'd been drinking, actually. At a party."

The woman inhaled. "I'm so sorry." She stopped. "You must—"

"I was actually trying to kill myself. I killed her instead, by accident."

It was like falling down the basement stairs, unexpected and unstoppable. Brent felt dizzy, unsure of where he was. He knew he hadn't let out this last fact before, not to his parents or the police or the psychologists. He felt empty inside, like a chicken from the store with its plastic bag of organs removed. He was glad the woman didn't know his name. He wanted to leave his confession, like his whirligigs, anonymously.

"It's hard to know what to say," the painter murmured. She set down her drink. They both stared out to sea. "From our chats, you certainly don't strike me as a killer. Or suicidal. Just look at your artwork." The wind toyed with the chimes and turned the row of pinwheels into blurs. "Only someone with a strong life force could possibly have created that."

The cicadas pulsed, then were silent.

"I'm sure you know that we all get depressed. Seriously, sometimes. Most of us probably think about throwing in the towel at some point." She paused. "And, God knows, we all make mistakes. All of the above, in my case." She looked at Brent. "I could be wildly wrong. But my sense of you is that you're a good person, not a bad one."

The words worked their way through Brent's brain. That he might in fact be like everyone else was a foreign idea, never considered. That he could have done what he'd done and still be good was an even more startling notion. He remembered the note from the motel maid: "No one is alone with Jesus." Jesus forgave you no matter what you'd done. But that was his business, and the priests' and ministers'. They were professional forgivers. They said "It's okay" the same way your parents said they loved you, whether they meant it or not. This, though, was different—hearing himself forgiven freely, by someone he trusted. He wasn't sure, though, that she knew enough to forgive him. He told her the story in detail. It didn't seem to change her mind.

The sun lowered toward the hills. Brent declined the woman's offer of dinner. He felt talked out. Producing the camera, he took four pictures of the whirligig from various angles and distances, the last one with the painter beside it. They exchanged farewells.

Brent continued into town. He bought groceries, then scented food coming from the diner nearby and decided he couldn't wait to eat until he made it back to the camp.

He stepped in and took a seat in the front corner, watching the comings and goings out the window as if he were in a trance. He couldn't quite believe the world was his to enter. He felt dazed and stayed on at his table long after his meal had been cleared. Across the street, cars were parking and people walking into the Town Hall. He paid, drifted out, heard music, and followed the others as if under hypnosis.

A pianist was pounding out chords on a stage, surrounded by a fiddler, a flutist, and a woman plucking a stand-up bass. Beside them, a gangling man was calling out steps to the two rows of dancers below. The music was brisk, bouncy, and infectious. Brent watched inconspicuously, leaning against the wall. Except for a few teenagers, the hall resembled a reunion of some sixties commune, with plenty of beards and ponytails in view. The caller's promptings, like an auctioneer's spiel, seemed almost to be in a foreign language.

"Allemand left. Now ladies' chain. Left-hand star. Back to the right. Actives down and back. Cast off. Everybody swing!"

Couples turned in circles, skirts rippling. Brent stared. It was a human whirligig, set in motion by music instead of wind. He sank into a chair and watched dance after dance. Suddenly, a young woman rushed up to him.

"We need one more couple." She held out her hands.

To his great amazement, he agreed. A few people clapped when he got to his feet. As before, the caller walked them through the dance slowly, without any music. Brent now recognized some of the steps. Knowing hands turned him left instead of right and pointed him toward the proper partner. Then the music started up at full speed and the dancers, like clock parts, began to turn. Arms reached for his. Faces whizzed past. He was instantly enmeshed with the others. Wordlessly they corrected him, adjusted his grip, smiled at him. He'd always been gawky. This hadn't changed. But the pattern of steps, repeated over and over, slowly began to sink in. The galloping tune had an Irish feel. It was exalting to be part of the twining and twirling, and strangely thrilling to touch other hands and to feel them grasping his. He felt like a bee returning to a hive, greeted and accepted by all. He clapped with the others when the music stopped, stood outside to cool off, and was promptly asked if he wanted to do the next one. His partner called the event a "contradance." It felt to Brent like his rite of reentry. He stayed all the way to the waltz at the end.

He slept late. When he woke, he could still hear the music and see the wide smile of the woman who'd driven him back. Birds were busy in the trees around him. He looked outside. The day was clear. He lay there for half an hour. Then he realized that he'd finished Lea's mother's task.

He built a fire and cooked himself some oatmeal, peering into the flames. The guilt hadn't magically vanished overnight. Four whirligigs wouldn't accomplish that. He knew it would reside in him like the ashes after a fire, unconsumed. But something had changed. He felt oddly buoyant. He discovered as well that a new view lay before his mind's eye. He saw himself returning to Chicago and to his parents. Delivering the photographs. Starting at a new school in the fall. These had been beyond the horizon until now. He began readying himself to meet them. He felt that he was up to it.

He put out his fire and packed his tent, then took out Lea's photo. It struck him now that the crash wasn't only something that he'd done to her. When they'd met, he was longing to be swallowed by the blackness. She'd set him in motion, motion that he was now transferring to others.

He replaced the photo and took out his bus pass. It didn't expire until August seventeenth. He had another three weeks left. He wouldn't mind seeing New Hampshire and Vermont. Then maybe camping on Lake George, in New York. Someone he'd met at the dance had just come back from a canoeing trip there. He thought he might build some more whirligigs. Maybe he'd start on a lifetime project of putting one up in every state.

He put on his pack and walked down to the office. He paid, then backtracked toward the cove, squinted, and made out his whirligig, bright against the painter's white house. The breeze off the water ruffled his hair and made the whirligig flash in the distance. He'd interlocked some of the propeller blades so that one would pass its motion to the others. In his mind, his whirligigs were meshed the same way, parts of a single coast-to-coast creation. The world itself was a whirligig, its myriad parts invisibly linked, the hidden crankshafts and connecting rods carrying motion across the globe and over the centuries.

He took off his pack. A few nights before, he'd come to the end of *Two Years Before the Mast*, the author's ship finally returning safely to Boston Harbor. He pulled out the book, felt linked with the writer and Emil and the others he'd met on the trip, and walked back inside the office. He placed it on the book exchange shelf, aware he was nudging an invisible gear forward. He wondered who would read it next. He scanned the titles and decided on *The Strange Lives of Familiar Insects*. Outside, a warm breeze ran its fingers through the trees. He started reading while he walked down the road.

Paul Fleischman is also the author of the Newbery Medal Winner *Joyful Noise* and the Newbery Honor Book *Graven Images*. He received the Scott O'Dell Award for *Bull Run*. Paul Fleischman lives in Pacific Grove, California.